A CASTLE LOST

Castle in the Wilde — An Early Days Novella

SHARON ROSE

Eternarose Publishing

Edited by: Light's Scribe Writer Services.

Cover design by: Kirk DouPonce, DogEared Designs

ISBN: 978-1-948160-27-8

To Jim and Marie,
who welcomed me with open arms.

CONTENTS

CHAPTER 1

S moke invaded his dream.

Thomas rolled over, coughing in the darkness. Too much smoke for a burning cottage or barn. What had his brothers done this time?

His family's stone keep could not burn. What was on fire? A half-moon glowed through the open window of his tower bedchamber, distorting the relief carvings in his mantel. He groped in its hazy light for the clothing and boots he'd cast aside, then dragged them on, almost tearing his fine shirt, still clammy with his sweat.

He opened the door and listened. The corridors of the keep were silent. He traversed one, following the stone with his hand until he reached the tapestry and the alcove behind it. Servants' stairs, but the fastest route to the wall. Where his father forbade him to go in darkness.

He needed no torch to descend these familiar steps. At the first landing, he twisted the iron latch and shoved the thick door open. No one challenged him. Where was the watchman?

More smoke. He darted down the short stretch of wall toward the corner tower, faintly lit by distant flames. He stopped short when the keep no longer blocked his view. Smoke billowed beyond the far castle wall, glowing orange above the village.

His throat constricted, and cold swept to his fingertips. What had— He swayed. His lungs demanded air. Thomas sucked in a ragged breath and tore himself from shock. He sprinted to the corner tower, crossed through it, then raced down the long wall, his boots pounding the stone.

A watchman jerked his head around and shouted, "Who goes?"

"Lord Thomas."

"The duke forbids you here at night."

"What then? Shall I hide in the keep while the village burns? What has happened?"

"I know not, but I'm not fool enough to cross Duke Kaituer. Go back."

"You didn't see me." Thomas darted past him and through the side gatehouse. Torches illuminated the smoke haze within.

Plenty of watchmen crowded beyond it, all drawn toward the east wall, where the virulent glow silhouetted the men-at-arms. They wouldn't let him through. What could he do anyway?

Something crashed, and a shower of sparks leapt high. Frantic screams. Wicked crackling. Waves of heat. Thomas muffled a cough in his shirt sleeve, his eyes stinging. Softer sounds reached him. Scuffling within the woods. Voices calling. Moaning sobs.

Would the forest catch fire too? How many would he find alive come dawn?

Esther! Her grandmother's house was half stone, but in that furnace heat...what chance the upper floor wouldn't catch? No menfolk to aid them. He couldn't leave his friend to burn.

Thomas bolted back into the gate tower and pounded down the curved steps. How to convince the keepers to open the gate?

No gatekeeper guarded it. Only Jacob. Good. He would understand, but his father was gatekeeper and would soon return.

"Open for me, Jacob. Then tell your father I went out and to let me in again."

Jacob gawked at him. "Master Thom—uh, Lord Thomas." He looked back and forth between Thomas and the open eye-slit in the gate. "My father went out to get our women from the village. He forbade me to open to anyone save him. Your brothers are out there, and the village men are swinging axes and pitchforks."

"They won't bother me. I have to make sure Esther gets out."

"I cannot. 'Tis a mad riot out there, and the duke will have my hide if I..." Jacob gave up his squawking as Thomas shoved the iron bars back.

He grabbed a torch from a bracket and thrust his shoulder against one side of the heavy, iron-strapped gate. "Lock it up. If villagers swarm near, do not open it."

He left the packed dirt for the grass, then made for the woods. Best to get into their cover soon in case Esther might be coming this way. Futility hit him. How could he find her in the dark woods? He glimpsed someone darting away from the light of his torch and shouted, "Have you seen Esther?"

"Nay." The lad scurried on by.

Once more he stopped to ask a fleeing woman who clutched two children. She shook her head, unable to speak over her coughing.

Everyone fled from the fire that he approached. If he could just reach her house at the edge of the village...at least see whether it stood.

Stand, it did. The sight almost emptied his stomach. Flames engulfed the upper walls. The stone-encased windows below glowed ruddy.

Where were Esther and her grandmother? No cries rose from the village now. Or did the inferno's roar mask them? What could he do?

'Twas then he made out faint sobs and followed the sound toward fluttering white fabric caught around a thin trunk. Nay, a person clung to the tree.

"Miss?"

She jerked her face toward him. "Thomas? Oh, Thomas!"

"Esther! Where is your grandmother?"

Her words were garbled, all squeaky.

He gave her arm a little shake. "Stop that and speak. Did she get out?"

Esther gasped and coughed. "She fell. I turned to help her, but she shouted, 'Run—don't look back.'"

A crash within the house ended hope. The upper floor must have collapsed, then the roof gave way. No time to comfort her. "We cannot wait." He grabbed her around the waist and half lifted her, turning back the way he had come. She wore nothing but a shift. He looked to her feet in the shadows. "Are those shoes?"

"Slippers of kid skin. I can make do."

He let go of her waist but took a firm grip on her hand. She ran to keep up, for his stride was now much longer than hers and he feared the fire might reach the forest. At least they had faint light from his torch, though its flames grew weaker as they hastened over hard ground. No matter, for he and Esther had run these paths in childhood…till he gained his title, and his father bade him to keep a proper distance from the village folk. The duke would not approve, but Thomas could not abandon a friend so dear.

They had nigh reached the main track to the castle when a voice whispered harshly, "Who goes?"

"Lord Thomas."

Jacob stepped into view. "Thank God." He matched their pace on Esther's other side.

"What are you doing out here?" Thomas demanded.

"Came to find you, of course, after my father got back with our women."

Thomas had thought only of Esther, but Jacob would have agonized over more. "Did he get all three of them safe to the castle?"

"Aye, but he's fair beside himself that you left."

"Not for long." Once they emerged from the woods, watchmen challenged them from the wall. Thomas used his voice and name to stay arrows. They ran over the grass, mostly carrying Esther between them. The gate swung open and soon slammed behind them.

Jacob's father shoved the iron bars into place. Over their scraping, he growled, "Your brothers are back. Get her out of sight."

Thomas shoved the torch into Jacob's hands and said, "Many thanks," as he darted into the tower.

Esther lurched. "Slow down!"

He had her by the waist again so she wouldn't fall, but... what was he doing? "Forgive me, I...I just want to get you safe."

"Aye, but these are big steps, and I can barely see."

He got her to the top without her tripping again. "Stay to my right as we cross the wall." 'Twas the best he could do to shield her white shift from view of anyone in the bailey. She ran with him. At last, he shut the door on the stairway landing inside the keep. "Hush." He listened. No footfalls on the stairs, nor flicker of light.

She trembled against his side. They'd always been comfortable together, but he'd never held her like this. 'Twas both wonderful and terrible. He whispered, "We're almost safe. These are straight stairs, one flight up. I won't let you fall."

She matched his steps.

At the top, he nudged the tapestry aside. All was still quiet and dark. They crept from behind it and trod softly along the corridor to his corner tower room. Inside, he closed and locked the door.

Scant relief here, overshadowed by...everything.

He took a firm step forward, then remembered that Esther knew nothing of this room. He nudged the sole chair so she could hear and maybe see its outline. "There's a chair here by the table. You can sit down while I light a candle." The tinderbox, he easily found in its accustomed place.

The flame sprang to life. A haze of smoke lingered in the air. Esther slowly looked around at the furnishings. Wardrobe, trunk, washstand, a tapestry hanging from a rod—all at odd angles in the circular room. The fireplace was small for the same reason. His rumpled bed stood out into the space, demanding attention. Which he'd never thought of before, but...how awkward it now seemed. He had a woman locked in his room. His throat squeezed too tight to speak, and the tail-end of fear left him shaky. Esther was shivering too.

Thomas opened the trunk and pulled out his winter blanket. He wrapped it around her, chair and all—that was also awkward —then sat on one of the stools by the fireplace. "I'm not like my brothers." What a stupid thing to say!

"I know you, Thomas. I'm not afraid of that."

She understood, of course. She always had. Everyone knew what sort his brothers were. At least they were half-brothers, so he didn't fully bear their taint. But he *was* a Kaituer. Anyone who discovered he had a woman in his room would think only one thing.

"I just..." She faltered. "I don't know what I'm going to do. And my gran—" Her face puckered. She folded over and sobbed into the blanket.

He had never seen anyone cry like that. Though he'd cried much the same way, alone in this room, the night his mother died. Had his father done so? The duke had just walked off to his bedchamber without a word and shut the door, while the maid sniffled beside the duchess's deathbed. How many folk were crying like this in the woods tonight? Worse, was it the fault of a Kaituer?

His brothers had burned barns for as little cause as the owner refusing to hide smuggled goods. For other things too, but he wasn't sure what. As a lad, he wasn't allowed in the private chamber beyond the hall, where the duke discussed plans with his sons. When he'd reached his eighteenth year... He had both hoped for inclusion and dreaded knowing what they really did. Though his father bestowed a ring and title upon him, and even commissioned his portrait, the duke had never summoned Thomas to join his brothers in that chamber. If they had anything to do with the village... His jaw jutted forward.

Esther's sobs waned to sniffs. Where was his brain? He found a clean handkerchief and gave it to her.

"Thank you," she muttered as she wiped her eyes and blew her nose.

He hated to ask, but he needed to. "Do you know...what started the fire?"

She flicked her eyes to his in a sullen look. "Not for certain, but I know what caused the fight beforehand, because I helped cook at the inn tonight."

She often did so. Her grandmother's family had once been prosperous, but time and illness had reduced their wealth to just the house. Now that was gone too.

Esther drew another breath. "Millie served the tables tonight, and she was talking about how it was her last time because she was getting married to the blacksmith's son in a few days. Your brothers were there, drinking too much like always. The host saw Lord Eustace eyeing Millie, so he told her to go home. Lord Eustace went right out after her as soon as she left. Folk noticed and went outside. I saw one of them running toward the blacksmith's place. In no time, your brothers were into it with the blacksmith, all four of his sons, and Millie's brothers. They had pitchforks and ran the three Kaituers right out of town. We would all have cheered if we dared."

"You weren't out in that mess, were you?"

"Nay, I watched from the inn. Then the host closed up early and had the stable hands walk me and Alice home. Everything quieted down. I went to bed and woke up to screams. The blacksmith's stable was ablaze, and over near Millie's place too."

Esther covered her face with her hands and rocked. "It spread so fast."

She couldn't seem to stop crying after that. He knelt on one knee beside her and tried to comfort her with a hand on her shoulder. Which only made her sob on his chest instead of the blanket. This wasn't working. Thomas hugged her close, slid an arm under her knees, and carefully stood. She was no heavier than a doe. He laid her on his bed, where sleep finally quenched her tears.

He stood by the open casement while stars faded in the graying sky above the distant tower trees. What was he going to do? A whole village destroyed. Too late to do anything about it. What would become of those poor souls in the woods? They were without shelter, clothes, food, or the means to get any of it. He looked at Esther. Her peace would end the moment she opened her eyes. She was safer than some, but not if his brothers saw her. At least he could get her clothes.

Thomas picked up the candle and left his tower room. He trod softly to the duchess's chamber. Nothing had changed here since she died, though an aged maid dusted it each Tuesday. Stealthily, he opened the wardrobe. Strange to look through his mother's gowns like this, but he withdrew a simple day gown. He opened the trunk with lifting shelves, which had fascinated him as a lad. What were all these linen things? He grabbed one of each, found stockings and shoes, then hurried back to his room. A distant door banged as he closed his own. The household must be rising.

He eased his bundle to the foot of the bed, careful to avoid Esther's feet. How was he going to hide her? He locked the door again. He'd have to open for the servant, but at least no one would barge in. Thomas untied the curtains bound to the bedposts. They would be conspicuous, for he never used them in summer, but he had to screen her somehow.

For all he pulled slow and steady, the rings scraping along the rods awakened Esther. She startled, then froze.

Thomas stepped back. "I didn't mean to wake you. I brought you some clothes." He pointed to the bundle, then went back to pulling the curtains around. "A servant will come with water and such. I'll have to let him in. Don't move or make one sound, and we just might be able to keep you hidden."

She nodded. "I...I'll dress as quick as I can."

Sounds issued from behind the curtains, many creaks of the bed and swishes of fabric. Fortunately, Esther finished before knuckles rapped on his door. Thomas opened it for the servant, who did indeed stare at the bed curtains. Before he could comment, Thomas said, "The night air grew vile. Do you know what happened?"

"The village burned. All of it. 'Tis naught but a smoldering ruin. The fields are blackened all the way to the stream."

Thomas feigned surprise. "All of it? How?"

"Everyone is blaming your brothers. By the look of Lord Eustace, he was in a brawl, sure enough. He won't be bragging anymore that he's the best looking Kaituer, not with his nose bent like it is. The duke's in a fine rage over the village. Servants are missing, too, which won't make him any happier when things don't get done."

"What a cheery day this will be. I'll not come down for breakfast. Bring me a tray and don't skimp, for I'm hungry."

In this way, he got Esther to eat. Sharing a simple repast at his table was an odd pleasure in a day of anguish.

They said little, but as Esther laid the fork on the empty plate they shared, she raised her blue eyes to his. "I thank you, Thomas."

He dipped his head but fumbled his reply. "I barely did a thing. Nor can I see my way to doing aught that matters."

"You gave me all I needed thus far." When he didn't answer, she rested her fingertips on the back of his clenched hand. "You gave me someone to trust."

That quick, the pressure in his chest lost its grip—only to tighten again when the door latch jerked.

He'd locked it, but he leapt to his feet as fast as Esther did.

A hard rap struck the door, and the duke's voice said, "Thomas?"

Esther went white.

"One moment, sir, until I'm decent," Thomas said. He pulled the tapestry outward and gestured to Esther. He'd hidden there once as a child. Was she small enough to fit against the curved wall without bulging the fabric?

She darted behind it, and he let go. The heavy tapestry fell straight.

He let a breath out and cleared his expression, then unlocked the door. He planned to stand in the doorway as he bowed. Instead, he hurriedly backstepped, for his father strode into the room and swung the door to bang into its frame.

The duke eyed the bare plate on the table. "Couldn't be bothered to come down to the hall?" His gaze ran up and down Thomas. "Are you injured?"

"Nay, sir. I had no part in the brawl."

His father's gray eyes narrowed. "Rumor has it that you were out during the fire."

"The smoke awakened me. I went to see if there was anything I could do, but the whole village was already in flames."

"Have I not forbidden you to go out in the night?"

"Should the son of a duke cower in his bedchamber?"

That worked. The deep creases below the duke's long nose eased a bit. He could no longer look down on Thomas, for they were eye to eye in height now. "If ever there was a night you should not have been seen, 'twas last night."

"What has the fire to do with Kaituers?"

"There was an uprising in the village last eve, and your brothers were beaten. Rebellions must be swiftly punished, or they spread."

"An uprising that my brothers started. All because Eustace won't keep his trousers tied, and the maid's family sought to protect her. For that, a whole village, and fields as well, should be burned? Or were they too drunk to think?"

Silence stretched before his father said, "They meant to burn only two houses, but you speak what I have not heard. How do you know, if you were not in it?"

He must not reveal Esther as the source. "I have ears," Thomas said with a shrug. "Is anyone talking of anything besides the fire?" His father's eyes narrowed again. Best not to wait for another question. "I daresay we'll soon run short of food. Servants are scarce, as well. Were some of them killed?"

"Some missing. Whether dead, hurt, or run off, I know not."

"I had thought of riding the woods," Thomas said, "for I know some villagers fled that way. I'll take Jacob with me."

"Head east first. Do not expect a warm welcome. Bid them gather near the north gate if they wish to return. Bring me word of what you are able to discover."

CHAPTER 2

Thomas closed the door behind his father, then pulled the tapestry's edge from the wall and whispered, "'Tis safe now."

Esther sidestepped from the narrow space, panting as though she'd held her breath. "I was so scared. What would he have done if he found me?"

"I would have spoken for you. Do not worry—he rarely comes to my chamber." Thomas urged her toward the chair. "The servants are the bigger problem. I'll tell them not to bother with my things in all this upset, but if anyone comes to the door, just duck behind the tapestry. We Kaituers have sharp eyes. If my father did not see any difference, no one else will."

Esther began undoing her thick, brown plait. After running for her life and sleeping on her braid, many a hair had escaped its confines. "Are you really planning to ride in the woods? For what?"

"I...I guess to see how bad things are. How many are out there...what they need."

"They shan't look well upon you. Best bring something to show good faith."

He almost demanded a reason why they would shun him. He

had always treated them decently. But he knew the answer. He was a Kaituer. Expected to become vile and ruthless. He unclenched his tight jaw. "What should I bring?"

"Almost anything. Clothes, shoes, food, blankets..." She looked around. "At the moment, I could use a comb."

He grabbed his from the shelf of the washstand and handed it to her. How was he going to get such things? He pulled his hunting jerkin on over his shirt, then strapped on his wrist guard. "I must go tend to things. Do not make a sound nor stand near the window." He picked up his quiver and bow from the angle between the wall and wardrobe. "I shall likely be gone some time. Do not fret."

She drew the comb through a lock of hair. "I will be fine." She didn't look like she believed that. When he hesitated, she dragged a smile up from somewhere and said, "I'll practice hiding as quick as a blink and...and make sure no sign of me exists anywhere."

Thomas nodded and slipped from the room. First, he raided a closet where bedlinens were kept, then he traversed back corridors and stairs. It didn't matter who saw him, but he had no patience for his brothers.

Jacob, he soon found in the gatekeeper's quarters beside the north side gate. Crowded now with Jacob's mother, sister, and young wife. They eyed the stack of blankets and sheets Thomas dropped on the table as they listened to his rough plan.

"That will never be enough," Jacob said.

"Nay, but all I could grab in the first load. I don't know where to get such things."

To Thomas's relief, Jacob's red-cheeked mother took charge of gathering, for she knew the castle workings. "I'll get some food that can travel and more blankets. May I use your name, Lord Thomas, to take what I need?"

"Aye." As they spoke, Jacob's father arrived and stood scowling in the doorway. His bristling eyebrows jutted more than usual. Thomas turned to him. "The duke knows I'm going out to see who I can find in the woods. He bade me tell the villagers they can gather by the north gate."

"Right, then," the matron said. "I'll bring everything back here, and you lasses will tie it up in packs, so it can be given out easy. We'll be quick as we can."

Thomas nodded. "Jacob, come to the stable with me."

Jacob matched his stride, looking all around before he whispered a question. "Esther?"

"Safe," Thomas said. "Later for that. We must ready horses, maybe one with a pack harness. I wouldn't mind hearing gossip in the stable."

"Then stay out of sight, while I saddle the horses."

Thomas didn't glean anything new, though Jacob tended to their mounts as slowly as possible. The sullen silence told its own story. The stable master was deep in the duke's smuggling operations, as were many stable hands. The lowly sort who shoveled the stalls kept their opinions to themselves.

When Thomas and Jacob led horses to the gatehouse, they found the collection of supplies to be meager.

The matron lifted one of the packets from a floppy basket. "Cheese and bread," she said. A rag was tied around it with a bit of twine. "These were all I could get. The steward was going around telling everyone that the duke has ordered food to be rationed, so then I couldn't get any more. I snuck as many winter blankets out of storage as I dared. Likely be a fuss come autumn if we can't get them replaced.

"Let's load them up," Thomas said. "We'll make do." Not enough, but he'd better get this all beyond the gate before someone stopped them.

This they did. He and Jacob began near the ruined village, riding back and forth. They wove eastward through the swath of ordinary forest that bordered Tower Woods. Folk had given that forbidding wilderness a wide berth. An eerie place, known only through mysterious tales, with trees so enormous that his tower room could have fit inside one tree trunk.

Survivors were difficult to spot, for they hid. Thomas began to suspect the reason. He fell back, following Jacob and the pack pony. Jacob had better success as he called out that he brought food and blankets. Never had Thomas hurt these folk, but they looked sideways when they recognized him. Easily done, for not many were as fair-haired as the Kaituers, and his nose was as long as his father's.

Then the food ran out. They continued on, giving a blanket to each huddled family. They handed the last one to a woman with three children. Her babe whimpered in her arms. As she asked Jacob whether he'd seen her husband, Thomas spied a wild goat standing still as a statue.

He slipped his bow off, nocked an arrow, and dispatched the goat with one shot. The woman and Jacob startled at the bow snap. Thomas rode through the bushes and retrieved the kill. He brought it back to the woman, and said, "This is for you."

She sneered at him. "Isn't that fine of you. As though I have a knife to gut it or a pot to cook it in."

Good point. "Jacob, clear a spot for a fire and get it lit for her." Thomas dismounted and tied his horse, then gutted and skinned the goat. By the time he finished, Jacob had sharpened some sticks for cooking. Thomas bent to a stream to rinse blood from his hands and spied a couple of weathered faces peeking through a distant bush. He nodded that direction. "Jacob, go tell those folk that we are friends and to come near."

The gray-haired couple approached, the woman in a nightdress, like so many, and the man wearing nothing but trousers.

Thomas had no food or blankets left. "All of my supplies are gone. I am so sorry. Jacob, leave the empty baskets here." Thomas drew his jerkin over his head as he spoke. "I know not what help baskets will be, but perhaps the babe may rest in one." He held the jerkin out to the elder. "You may have this."

The man stared for a moment, then took it with a bow. "I thank you, Lord Thomas."

Thomas returned a jerky nod, swallowing hard. He mounted and rode away. Jacob soon caught up, leading the pack horse. From the corner of his eye, Thomas caught Jacob looking at him, but his friend didn't speak. Just as well. Thomas had cooled his expression, but his insides boiled. In this moment, he hated his brothers. Words he could never say, for the duke had silenced every scrap of bickering among his sons with a stern lecture on solidarity. The only time they'd felt his rod was when they fought with each other. The Kaituers were a clan as solid as their stone castle.

Thomas and Jacob rode south through the woods to reach the road that would take them home the fastest. Through the trees, Thomas spotted horses, a wagon, and—was that a lady? How awkward to be wearing naught over his shirt. They left the woods for the road and faced the cavalcade that had stopped there. A man stood in the wagon and distributed something to a gathering of folk clad in nightwear. Doubtless, more impoverished villagers.

The lady saw Thomas and turned her horse, riding nearer. The ample folds of her riding habit swayed a foot above the ground. Her silver-streaked hair was impeccably coiled. She rode with such dignity that her horse seemed like a portable throne.

She halted a few yards away, and Thomas bowed slightly from the saddle. "Good day, Lady Eberle."

She granted him neither title nor the faintest inclination of her head. "Well, well. If it isn't a Kaituer. What brings you out? The opportunity to gloat over your victims?"

"Nay, to bring supplies to those who lost homes when a fire chanced to spread."

"Chanced? A fire that you started."

"You are misinformed, lady. I did nothing of the sort." He fumed inside. His brothers should be taking these insults.

She angled her head to view the extra horse with an empty pack harness. "You seem to be rather short of supplies. Indeed, 'tis quite strange that you must come all this way to find your people. I cannot help but wonder why they did not flee into the castle."

"Some did. The rest are welcome to return."

"Mm. They don't seem to know that. But worry not, I have given them food and offered them a safe haven at Eberle Manor."

"As I have done to the west of here, so all are now attended to. I suggest you return to your home, Lady Eberle."

"How like your brothers." She huffed through her nose. "Your mother had hopes you would be different. She must be turning in her grave." The lady reined her horse around and ambled toward her retinue.

Thomas turned likewise and trotted westward. What, exactly, made her say that? His father didn't like her, but...had his brothers ordered her off their property before? Why must he bear this comparison? If anything, he had been more courteous than she had.

Jacob finally spoke. "What was that all about?"

"I wish I knew."

Silence stretched again, then Jacob said, "You never told me about Esther."

"I wanted to be sure no one would hear. I got her up to my tower room without anyone knowing, but I'm going to have a terrible time keeping her hidden. I would ask your mother to take her in, though now that you're all squashed together in the gatekeeper's room, I cannot."

"Nay, we can scarce breathe."

"At least the servants are spread too thin to bother me much. I had another idea, and in part, I was thinking how to arrange this even before the fire."

"What?"

"I'm old enough to have a squire now. Not that I'm sure what I need one for, but...if you're willing to be squire to a Kaituer...I could make it so you are the only one who enters my room. Then, I'd have two things I want at once. What think you?"

Jacob let out a whispery laugh. "I won't serve just any Kaituer, but I'd be happy to serve you."

Thomas grinned. Hard to believe something good had happened today. "'Tis done, then. Now let us hasten. Lady Eberle worries me, and I would tell my father."

They cantered the remainder of the way and entered the castle through the north gate. No one from the village lingered nearby.

Another guard was on duty, and as he slid the bars into place, Thomas asked, "Have any villagers come to this gate?"

"Some families of those employed here. Why?"

"Just curious. Jacob, take the horses to the stable, then come up to my chamber."

CHAPTER 3

Thomas crossed the bailey toward the keep, built by generations long gone. An imposing edifice of gray stone, as wide as it was tall, with a tower jutting from each of its four corners. Lower windows were no more than a foot wide, with three rows of stately, double-arched windows above. Thomas reached the central steps and climbed them. A guard stood on duty at the entrance—unusual. He opened the thick, iron-strapped door and bowed as Thomas passed him.

In the hall, Thomas caught sight of a tray of bread and cheese that remained on the raised head table. His stomach rumbled as he strode to it. One servant still labored to clean trestle boards after the noon meal.

"Where is Duke Kaituer?" Thomas asked as he tore off a hunk of bread.

The servant tilted his head to the doorway behind the raised table. "Yon with Lord Arthur."

"Leave this tray here for me and bring fruit and meat."

Thomas went to rap on the door of the duke's private chamber, so named because no one could enter without his expressed permission. No servant could even clean it unless the duke were present. "'Tis Lord Thomas," he said, loud enough to be heard through the stout door.

A voice called from within. "Enter."

He did so, then swung the door shut.

An austere chamber, with no cushion upon any surface, not even Duke Kaituer's high-backed chair at the table. 'Twas sparsely furnished for such a spacious room. A few chests and a tall cabinet flanked the fireplace. The only adornments were weapons mounted on the walls, and a silver candelabra on the heavy table. Thomas bowed to his father, who was pacing, with a hand resting on his sword hilt. Unlike him to pace. Not a word did he speak.

Thomas took another bite of the bread in his hand as he neared the table, where Arthur sat watching him over the rim of his tankard. He looked sour, his head likely throbbing from the bruise that spread across the side of his forehead and merged into his blond hair.

Thomas poured ale from a pitcher into a tankard, then washed down the bread.

Arthur sneered. "Someone steal your clothes, little brother?"

"Nay. I gave my hunting jerkin to a village father who— thanks to my wise elder brothers—had greater need of it than I."

"Young fool. Pander to them, and they will—"

"Hold your tongue," the duke snapped. He halted beside the table, his boots striking hard on the stone floor. "How far did you travel in the woods, and what did you learn?"

Thomas leaned over the map spread on the far end of the table, sweeping his hand over an area as he answered. "I crisscrossed from the village, heading east, and ended about here."

"Is that as far as they spread?"

"I think not. Some may have fled west, but still, I didn't find even a tenth of the village folk. I told them they could come to the castle, but they are not returning. They're afraid—even of me."

"Why didn't you ride farther?"

"Partly because I'd run out of anything to give them, and partly bec—"

"Give them?" Arthur demanded.

Thomas braced his hands on the table and leaned toward his brother. "I gave them blankets and a scant bit of food. They're wandering around hungry in their night clothes, trying to find their families with no idea whether they lived, because you burned their homes."

"They took up steel against us."

"Because you—"

"Enough!" the duke said. "Know this, Thomas. No matter the provocation, the commoners cannot be allowed to rise against us and win."

"I know the law, sir, but we did not win either."

Though his father closed his lips, Arthur declared, "We did!"

"Not so," Thomas said, his voice a calm contrast to his eldest brother's. "When you burn everything down—*no one* can live there." He leaned nearer. "Not your enemies. Not your allies. Not even you."

Arthur cast a glowering look from Thomas to his father. Had he heard the same thing from their sire? He cursed and said, "We never meant it to spread so far."

"Fire is like that," Thomas said. "Once lit, it grants no mercy to friend or foe."

"We—"

"In this, your brother speaks true." The duke's glare shut Arthur's mouth. "If word of this reaches the king, we will feel the fire of his rage."

"It likely will," Thomas said. Their eyes turned to him. "I met Lady Eberle soon after I ran out of supplies."

"Where?" Arthur demanded as the duke asked, "In the woods or on the road?"

Thomas pointed at the map again. "About here, on the road.

Her attendants had a cart, and they were giving food to our villagers."

Arthur shoved his chair back and stomped away from the table. "That is our land."

"The road is open to all," the duke said.

"But she was dealing with our—"

"Be silent." The duke turned back to Thomas. "What words did you exchange?" He listened to the answer, then asked, "Did any of her people draw arms against you?"

"Nay, sir. One held a bow and watched steadily, but he didn't have an arrow nocked. Jacob and I were still on our land, not hers, and we were only wearing our bows. They had neither right nor need to draw. Indeed, the lady rode away from her men to approach me. 'Twas not as though she feared, for all she disdains. Why does this matter?"

"She has come prying about on our land before," Arthur said. "Seeking to stir trouble. We ordered her to stay away."

"What trouble can she stir?"

"That is not your concern," the duke said. "Where is Jacob? I don't want him spreading this about."

"Stabling the horses before he returns to me." Thomas inclined his head. "With your leave, sir, I would have him as squire."

"Be off, then, and see that the captain knows."

Obvious that his father was thinking of matters far weightier than the appointing of a squire. Thomas half wanted to know what, but better to leave when dismissed. Besides, he was hungry, and Esther must be too. The tray still awaited him in the hall, with the extra food he'd ordered. He carried it up three flights of stairs and along the corridor to his corner tower.

Jacob was hovering near the door, looking uncomfortable.

Thomas handed him the tray. "What is wrong?"

"Nothing. I just don't know what to say if someone asks what I'm doing here."

Thomas fit the key in the lock. "Bear yourself as befits my

squire and answer accordingly. I told the duke my wish, and he concurred, so it is done." Jacob squared his shoulders, as Thomas swung the door inward. No sign of Esther. "Jacob, set that on the table." Thomas shut the door with a distinct snap. "You can come out, Esther."

The tapestry wiggled, and she emerged. "I'm so glad you're back."

By the way her gaze snagged on the tray, she needed food more than him. "Sit down and eat." Thomas took the stool again. "Jacob, did you find some food for yourself?"

"Aye. My wife had a bite set aside for me. I stopped into the gatekeeper's quarters before I came up."

Esther shook her head. "Once folk take on work in the castle, they half disappear. I heard you'd married, Jacob, but not whose hand you took."

"Johanna accepted me. She grew up within these walls. Her father is the tanner, and her mother, the chandler."

"Why don't I know her? Does she never go out?"

"She is a shy one, more likely to go hunting bees in the woods than ribbons in the village market."

Esther's brows darted together as she dipped her head.

"I...I'm..." Jacob floundered.

She straightened. "I keep trying to think of something else, but it doesn't work." She met Thomas's eyes. "Please tell me what you discovered in the woods."

They shared the names of the destitute folk they'd found and given scant aid to. Jacob told the part about the goat and jerkin, which made Esther smile upon Thomas.

He couldn't think of how to respond to that, but he must keep Jacob from speaking of who they'd met next. "Since we had nothing else to give," Thomas said, "and my father was waiting to hear from me, we rode home. Besides, I've worried all day what to do for you. To start with, Jacob is my squire now."

She gave Jacob a smile and nod, for she was kind that way.

"I wanted him as squire anyway," Thomas said. "Then, I

realized I could make it so that only Jacob waits on me. I thought you might feel safer that way. You will, won't you? I mean, I know we're grown now, but we were always friends."

She nodded, though her lips quivered like she just might cry.

"Certain, she is safe," Jacob said, "for I have it on good authority that a squire never dishonors his lord's lady."

Esther's eyes flitted about. She grabbed a pear from the tray and took a hasty bite.

Thomas glared at Jacob.

"'Tis only fair that she knows, sir, especially now that everything has gone awry." To Esther, Jacob said, "I was at the gate last night when Lord Thomas went out. 'Twas only the name of Esther that was on his lips."

She swallowed her bite of pear. "I…I am not a noble lady, though, and Lord Thomas will marry a true lady. We must not let ourselves pretend, for Duke Kaituer will never look upon the likes of me for his son."

All that she said was true—and wrong. There was not a word in his brain that Thomas could utter.

"I never doubted," Esther said, "that he came for me, for Thomas has ever been my truest friend. Let this friendship always remain, lest my broken heart shatter any worse."

"It shall remain," Thomas said. His stomach churned. Still hungry, but now he couldn't eat. "I never meant that you should stay…permanently…in my room. Jacob, find a moment to drop a word in your mother's ear this eve, that we need a safe place for Esther to dwell." Even as he said the words, he doubted such a place existed. Not with so many of the smugglers residing in the castle. "For tonight, Esther, you will be safer here. I'll be out most of the eve, for I must soon go down to dinner in the hall, and I want time to hear what's being said."

They both nodded to him. Jacob didn't move. He was good with horses and had taught Thomas everything he knew of hunting, but in the keep, he was going to need a lot of help.

"Jacob," Thomas said, "when dinner nears, fetch hot water up from the kitchen so I may wash and change my clothes."

That got him out the door.

Thomas stood and paced a little. He ought to be saying something. "Uh, you tidied my room." Quite the conversational gambit.

"I got bored," Esther said. "No one of the household could get in, nor did any even try. While I made the bed, I noticed a pallet underneath it."

"Aye, for a servant." He knew well that it couldn't be seen. She had looked for it, but he didn't mind.

Her eyes narrowed. "Fine. I was snooping. They are common enough, and I hoped you had one. I can sleep on it tonight. The bedcurtains provide a screen, so we can have a little privacy."

"That, they do, but I will sleep on the pallet."

"Nay, Lord Thomas, you are—"

"If you're going to call me *lord*, then you shouldn't be arguing with me. You must know that a title makes a person autocratic."

She huffed. "You've always told me what to do. Tried to anyway."

That little toss of her head showed that she was jesting. Even today, she gave him reason to smile. "This argument, I will win. How far did you snoop?"

"Not near as far as I wanted to. Oof, 'twas boring. Not a stitch to be set, nor a word to be read, and likely just as dull once you go down to dinner."

He went to the trunk, opened it, and took out the only book it held. "This was my mother's. All the other books are down in the library." He set it on the table.

Esther traced the engraving on the leather cover. "A holy book." Her lips formed an odd quirk. "I wonder how many would believe such a book could be found in this castle."

"Those who knew my mother would believe it." Lady Eberle's words returned to him. Certain, she didn't believe his mother's virtue had done *him* any good. What an infernal mess everything was.

Jacob soon returned with hot water, and Esther sat down at the table with her back to him, apparently engrossed in the book, while he readied himself for dinner.

Suitably clad, Thomas went down to the hall and managed to get a few minutes of conversation with the captain. When his father arrived, Thomas went to take his place at the raised table, where the duke's sons always sat, two on either side of him. Being the youngest, Thomas sat second to the left. Not tonight. Arthur took his normal seat on his father's right, but Rupert sat next to Arthur, and the duke motioned Thomas to the place at his left. The third plate for Eustace was set beyond Rupert, though he had yet to put in an appearance. Hiding his broken nose, most likely. Why did his father separate his elder three sons from the youngest?

Jacob served him tonight, watching the other squires and copying them. Always, a single servant had waited on Rupert first, then Thomas. Certain, he was elevated to sit next to the duke. Yet he felt oddly...set apart.

Why?

Almost as puzzling as that question, the long trestle boards of the hall did not fill as usual, even with additional villagers taking empty places. A silent gathering, which dispersed with unusual haste. Perhaps the duke's forbidding mien caused it. When the duke turned that expression to Thomas, he felt sure of it.

"You will retire to your tower room now and *stay* there, this night."

Thomas bowed. "I shall, sir."

CHAPTER 4

Not one of Thomas's brothers joined them in the hall the next morn when he broke his fast at his father's side. 'Twas almost as ominous as the duke's brooding silence and his curt order that Thomas was to stay within the keep. What was going on?

He went first to the library. Not that he could read in all this turmoil. Instead, he grabbed a couple volumes and hastened up the steps to his tower room. His mother had decreed that this would be his bedchamber—'twas well separated from his brothers' chambers. Even that puzzled him more than usual today. He had not locked the door this time, so he tapped the signal knock they had agreed upon, then entered.

Even still, Esther stood wide-eyed when he opened the door, her fingers frozen amidst hair and ribbon. Then her face relaxed, and she continued passing ribbon through her braided locks, fastening them in a coil around her head. The flat basket of hair trimmings that he had smuggled from his mother's chamber was nowhere to be seen. Nor any other hint of her sojourn.

"Did you get any breakfast?" he asked.

"Aye, Jacob brought it up. I cleaned the plate and hid it in your trunk."

He set the books on the table. "At least I needn't worry you'll give anything away with carelessness."

"As long as no one notices missing things. In addition to my gown and ribbons, I have now purloined an eating knife, hidden away within my pocket."

He tried to grin at her saucy tone and said, "Call nothing stolen. I have given you each item."

"What is the matter, Thomas? You look more troubled than when you left."

"I don't know. My father bade me remain within the keep, and there were even fewer folk in the hall this morn than there were at dinner last eve."

"Are folk...leaving?"

Thomas shrugged. "It looks that way, but Jacob might know more. Where is he?"

"He left to give me privacy." She tied the ribbons at the nape of her neck. "Thank the heavens, he took that smelly chamber pot with him!"

She was trying to get him to laugh. Not working. "If folk are leaving, we can maybe find you a different place to stay, but I fear to let you stay alone. Someone will notice, and half the men within the castle walls cannot be trusted." He ground his teeth. "Much like half the men within the keep."

Her gaze fell. Her lips moved as though they held words she couldn't say. She stepped past him, giving his arm a touch on the way, then sat down by the table. "Perhaps..." Still, she could not say whatever it was. "What did you bring me to read?"

He lowered himself to a stool, rested his arm on the table, and looked into her blue eyes. So pretty, and the little black dot below the outer corner of one eye somehow made them even prettier. Which would not make her safer. "We need to...figure something out for you. Prepare, at least."

"I know. I'm not even sure if I should stay in the castle or try to find friends outside...but that could be dangerous, too, and no one will have any means to help another." She plucked at her gown. "I'm probably the wealthiest villager, as it is."

He understood what she didn't say. In truth, she had nothing but clothes...and an eating knife. No meat to cut unless he or Jacob snuck it to her.

She fumbled through the gown's slit to her pocket tied within. "Anyway, I...I hope this is not too presumptuous, but I made a list on a scrap of parchment I found in your trunk. They are things I would need in order to get started on my own again." She handed it to him. "If I had needles, sheers, and thread, I could perhaps sew for folk and..."

He clasped her hand, his eyes lowered to the list. "You've no need to explain. I will give you whatever you request and coin too. It is your safety that worries me. Even if all were well in the village, you would not have left your grandmother's home until you had a husband's protection."

"Aye, well...that isn't going to be done in a day, now is it?"

They both heard it in the same instant...a hard stride approaching.

Esther snatched the list from his fingers and darted behind the tapestry a bare second before the door opened. Thomas positioned himself so he appeared to have risen from the chair and bowed to his father.

The duke slammed the door. "Where is your squire?" His words were clipped and harsh.

"I assume he is off wherever chamber pots are emptied."

"As soon as he returns, bid him to pack for a hunting trip of several weeks. Take your Kaituer sword and dagger, as well as your bow. I want you in Tower Woods until...things settle."

Tower Woods? "Wh...uh...why?"

The duke paced before the fireplace. A relief Esther wasn't hiding beyond the bed. "Your brothers *escorted* Lady Eberle to the castle and quartered her in one of the guard towers."

Thomas could hardly breathe. He managed to utter, "Against her will?"

"Need you ask?"

"Nay, but...surely 'tis madness."

"Young Lord Eberle certainly takes strong exception to it. He is beyond the main gate, demanding his mother's immediate release. He has scattered his men round about the castle, but fortunately, does not have enough—yet—to do anything but watch the gates. By tomorrow's dawn, he will discover how vulnerable his men were in darkness. By then, you and your squire will be in Tower Woods, where you will remain until I know what action the king will take against us." He halted and seemed to consider the contents of his son's room. "Be sure to take all that you need to live off the...woodland."

That last word slowed, and the duke's gaze fixated where the tapestry met the floor. His brows rose.

Thomas couldn't help but follow his gaze. The hem of Esther's gown peeked from below the tapestry.

Ah, the ice that the duke could put into quiet words. "Aren't you going to introduce me to the woman who shares your chamber?"

"Only if I may request your forbearance," Thomas said as he crossed in front of the tapestry and drew the edge forward. He took Esther's hand in a firm grip, drawing her gently from the alcove. "For Esther has been my friend since childhood, and she lost her home and family when the village burned."

She spread her skirt and curtsied low, murmuring, "My lord duke."

The duke's face went rigid. "You are wearing my wife's gown."

"I gave it to Esther," Thomas said, "for she had naught but a shift when I rescued her. I made sure it was one that Mother sewed for herself, so it could not have been a gift from you. I am heir to my mother's property, so the gown is mine to give."

Esther stood immobile, her hands clenched at her waist, but her gaze steady as the silence lengthened.

"What is your family name," the duke finally asked.

"Harnon," she said. Certain, she must be frightened, but her voice was so clear that Thomas felt proud of her. "My father was—"

"I know your family," the duke said. "Your father studied law before his untimely death, and your uncle was once priest in the village."

"That is true," she murmured.

"Have you a husband, or are you yet a maid?"

As if it were not shocking enough that the duke knew of her family...what sort of question was this?

"N-nay, my lord duke. That is...I am a maid. I lived with my grandmother, but...the house collapsed...she didn't escape."

"There are worse fates than a quick death," the duke said. Esther swallowed loudly, but he continued. "She could not have endured life in the woods. Nor will you survive without a husband."

"Sir..." What to say after that, Thomas had no idea, but at least the duke turned his gaze upon him.

The pointed hush of his father's voice accentuated his next words. "There will be certain difficulties in obtaining brides for my sons anytime soon."

Thomas still had no words as he took in his father's meaning. A gentle, coded knock struck the door, and the duke raised his brows in question. "That is Jacob...my squire."

"Enter."

Jacob must have recognized the duke's voice, for he bowed as he opened the door.

"How old are you?"

Jacob's brow twitched. "Twenty, my lord duke."

"Have you a wife or a favored one who would take your hand this day?"

"A...a wife, sir. The tanner's daughter, Johanna."

"Fetch her up to this room, at once. She will become maid to Lord Thomas's wife."

Jacob's mouth dropped open, but he bowed and left.

When the door shut, Thomas said, "Father, what are you doing?"

"Ensuring heirs to the House of Kaituer. I have enemies in the duchy who carry tales to King Carleeton. Then, he blames me that they vanish. His last warning was…harsh in the extreme. I must get you away. I do not know when I will see you again. *If* I will see you again. Thus, you will be wed this day in the chapel before witnesses, so that no one can say your children are illegitimate. You must still flee into Tower Woods. That is of far greater import than a wedding ceremony, so bend your mind to that."

The duke turned sharply to Esther. "You will soon be Lady Esther. You may take what you need from Lord Thomas's inheritance in his mother's chamber. Be wise in your choices, for you must carry everything on a pack horse and it must sustain you for months to come."

To Thomas, the duke said, "Be in the chapel by noon. I must find the priest."

Esther's breathing was loud in the silence left by the duke's departure. So white, she was, that Thomas put an arm around her and guided her to sit in the chair. He closed the door, then considered the dazed look on her face. His own bemused sensation was passing. How long would it take her? Outrageous of his father. And yet… He didn't mind at all. Did Esther?

Thomas returned to the stool before her. She was silent. Ominous. She always filled the gaps when he didn't know what to say. He licked his lips. "I won't let him force you into it."

"Do we…have a choice?"

"He won't give us one, but we can always make our own. If you don't want to do this, I will sneak you away this very moment, but…I know it is a lot to ask. Off to Tower Woods, for months maybe, when you're used to a solid house."

Her mouth did an odd quivery thing. "Truth be told, the castle scares me more than Tower Woods. I was trying to think how I could tell you that I dared not stay here. 'Cept, I'm afraid to be alone too."

"Then if..." Wait, he wasn't supposed to ask this perched on a stool. He shifted forward to one knee. "If you would be pleased to join hands with me, 'twould make me happy all of my days, whether we dwell in a woodland or a castle."

She drew a breath and let it out with the sweetest smile she'd ever bestowed on him. "Me too." She extended her hand, and he took it.

Now what? Was he supposed to kiss her fingers? He wasn't sure, but...that seemed like a wonderful idea. So he did, and she smiled again.

He stood up—if anything, more bemused than when his father left.

She stood too. "It's a good thing I made a list, isn't it?"

"Aye. Today is even stranger than yesterday." He clapped a hand to his forehead and groaned. "I didn't mean...that's not what I meant to say."

"Well, it is, though, so you may as well say it."

Jacob's knock sounded, and Thomas bade him enter. Jacob darted a glance around the room, looked relieved, then drew his wife within. Even as he shut the door, he blurted out, "The castle is surrounded by Lord Eberle's men, for his mother is locked in the guard tower. Your brothers...the duke... What is going on?"

"My brothers have gone madder than ever, and my father believes the king will act against us. He is sending me to Tower Woods to hide until..." He flung a hand wide. "I don't know when. He decided in a matter of seconds that Esther is to marry me and you two must accompany us into...I can only call it exile."

They just stared at him.

"I can't blame you if you refuse. Um..." He drew Esther's hand unto his arm. "After my father left us, Esther accepted my offer of marriage and to flee with me to Tower Woods. I, we, do hope that you will come with us."

"Well, I am your squire." Jacob looked at Johanna. "This castle is the last place I want to leave my wife." She gave him a quick nod, and Jacob said, "So we are with you."

"Right, then. We have a hundred things to do. A wedding at noon, and we depart at nightfall. At least, we needn't hide you anymore, Esther. I'll take you and Johanna to my mother's chamber. Then Jacob and I will see to provisions."

CHAPTER 5

Would he even remember his wedding? So rushed it had been. Somehow, Thomas paid attention during the vows and when he slipped his mother's ring onto Esther's finger. Perhaps he would remember, too, the look in her wide blue eyes. They turned to him again now, as he helped her into the saddle. Too dark to see the color though.

Seven ponies stamped beside the gate. A couple hands shorter than the horse he left behind. These were sturdy horses, known for strength and surefootedness. No more would they bear the smuggled goods hoisted up the cliffs by the sea. Instead, they would bear a lord and lady into exile. Thomas wished they had no smuggler with them now, but the duke had ordered one of that band to guide them into Tower Woods. A foul-toothed fellow named Rufin, with an annoying habit of spitting.

The second runner to return to the gate spoke hushed from beyond the open eye-slit. "All's clear."

This was it. The men mounted. The last bar of the gate was slid aside as quiet as could be. The gate opened, and Rufin led them out single file—across grass and in among the nearest trees.

How quiet these ponies. Trained for that, perhaps, and their hooves unshod. Through the night, they followed trails northwest, or so Thomas assumed. He could do nothing except check repeatedly that the others did not lag and strain his eyes to keep Rufin's back in view. A man he didn't trust. They were well beyond their hunting lands now. Did Rufin even know where he was going?

They halted at last. "Wait here," Rufin said. "I must find it."

Thomas tilted his head back until his gaze reached starlight beyond the distant treetops, straight above him. 'Twas Tower Woods. "Find what? We are here."

"Fah. The entrance." Rufin spat and rode away.

Why did one need an entrance to a woodland? Were they not in forest already, even though 'twas rocky in this stretch? Jacob rode forward from his place at the rear to see why they lingered, then speculated on the likelihood that their guide had abandoned them.

Yet Rufin returned and led them on, down into a vale, which narrowed between...what were these walls made of? Dirt banks, perhaps, for plants brushed Thomas's shoulders. The air changed. Moist, with scents he didn't recognize.

Rufin halted again. "Dismount here."

Thomas did so and passed the word back, then followed Rufin, who seemed to be waving a stick high before him. It struck something.

"Best watch your head, Lord Thomas, tall as you are."

Thomas soon found the obstacle with a raised hand. Wood, curving lower.

"What is it?" Esther asked faintly.

"The underside of a fallen trunk." The surface continued unnaturally—far too broad, with little curve. A tower tree.

Rufin must have tied his pony, for he worked his way back and made sure the two pack-laden ponies got under.

Was the sky beginning to gray? Hard to tell. Thomas spotted Rufin's pony and headed that way. He nearly fell as his boots slipped over uneven ground. At least there was more space than in the passage. Over his shoulder, he said, "Hang tight to your saddles and test your steps."

Rufin returned and untied his mount. "This is where I leave you. Wait here until the sun rises enough to see your way."

"Which direction is the trail?"

Rufin scoffed. "There is no trail. Head north to get further in, south to get out. Likely the duke will send me to find you when things settle down. If you hear the call of an owl, but it lilts up, that's me." He cupped his hands around his mouth and demonstrated. "I'm off, then." He led his pony back under the fallen trunk, his sound soon lost as well.

Darkness and rustling silence engulfed them. Thomas had never felt so lost. Where were they, or where could they go? Those tales he had heard... What nocturnal animals moved about? Were they dangerous? He could neither defend, nor flee, nor even sit down.

Nigh breathless, Esther asked, "What do we do?"

He'd better quit floundering around in his own confusion. "We settle ourselves here to wait out the night. The horses need to rest, anyway."

Jacob murmured to Johanna, and she began fumbling her way to him.

Esther took a couple steps toward Thomas and fell. Branches shifted beneath his boots as he tried to reach her. She managed to drag herself upright with the aid of a stirrup leather.

"Are you hurt?"

"I twisted my ankle." How shaky her voice. "I daresay it will be fine in a moment or two."

He finally got close enough to grip her elbow...to feel her trembling. "Just stand still for a minute, while I find you a place to sit." There had to be a log or root or rock or *something*!

He slipped his bow off his shoulder and used it to prod about while Jacob tied horses. Dishonorable use for his fine bow, but he found a thick root where he could perch and hold Esther in his lap. Johanna insisted that Esther rest her injured foot upon Johanna's knee, and thus they awaited dawn in awkward rest.

The sloped root soon inflicted pure torture on Thomas's spine. Though the night was not cold, the damp air chilled them. Esther slowly went limp against his chest. His arms ached, for he must support her. This scant bit of rest was all he could offer her. What a horrible wedding night. How could he have been fool enough to bring a bride into his nightmare?

Fog slowly lightened in the dawn. It shrouded ominous shapes and dark pillars. Ferns took form in the whiteness. Esther awoke and stared at their surroundings.

"My dear one," he said, "I must stand."

"Of course—'tis fine."

She found a branch to grip as he bent this way and that, trying to work out the aches. She favored one foot. Not good, but her face seemed clear of pain. Mesmerized, in fact, as she gazed high and low. Now that he could see the ground, Thomas realized they stood on a jumble of deadwood caught amidst rocks. There must be more stable ground, though he saw none at hand. What a wild, unlivable place. Jacob frowned too, dampening a handkerchief with a few drops from his waterskin and wiping Johanna's face. Had she wept in silence during the night?

Thomas tried to find words adequate for the apology he owed them all, but Esther's voice interrupted, awe thrumming in each syllable. "'Tis beautiful!"

What? He looked again...all around. Mist rose in wisps, a lazy dance through shafts of sunlight. Dew-flecked greenery covered branches and grew from a rotting trunk. "I...I suppose it is." He surveyed it a moment longer. "I wish it could make up for...to all of you for what my—"

She pressed a hand against his chest. "It doesn't need to make up for anything. 'Twas a dreadful night, but we have survived it and will do better now."

"Well said." Jacob began tightening the saddle girths he'd

loosened when they'd stopped. "I suggest we look for a place to eat and get a few hours of sleep, then head north and make a real camp before the sun sets."

"Aye, there must be a better place than this." If Thomas could just find it. Now that he could see a few hundred yards through the mist, he discerned some ordinary trees among the tower trees. Comforting, though he didn't know why. He jerked his head toward one of them. "I'll head over there and climb a bit, to get a better view." Scrounging near his feet, he found a stout bit of wood to use as a walking stick and set off.

Once he got past the scrambled branches of the dead tree they'd spent the night on, going grew tolerable—barely. By the time he reached his goal and ascended a few limbs, Jacob had the women mounted and the pack ponies tied to saddles. They followed the route he'd taken with a good deal of fumbling. This journey was not going to be easy. He'd best study the northward land carefully.

When Jacob reached him, he climbed down. "I think that's a game trail through there." He pointed. "In case you didn't notice, the obstacles are going to weave us around in endless loops. We've got to have a goal, so I'm picking that tree with the broken *V* branch caught in the limbs. Do you see it?"

Jacob grimaced. "Slim chance a game trail will lead to it, but better than nothing."

They didn't reach it, but at least they kept setting new northward goals. An hour must have passed before they stopped, exhausted, in a place that yielded some comfort. They ate dried meat and bread, then stretched out on the ground. Thomas knew he wouldn't be able to sleep with all this misery, but...

THOMAS OPENED gritty eyes when a shaft of sunlight crept past a limb and fell onto his face.

Only Esther was awake. Her smile was so wan that he pulled

her close to his chest. Oh, for words to comfort her, but there were none. At least she breathed easy, her chest rising and falling in a soothing rhythm beneath his hand, until Jacob and Johanna stirred.

They traveled again, stopping at every climbable tree, from which Jacob or Thomas searched again and again for a space to make camp. Finally, Thomas spied a site, and they reached it before the sun sank too low. They augmented their packed food with a few squirrels roasted over a small fire, and though there was no shelter for them, the two couples found comfortable spots to sleep.

If only distant voices shouting curses didn't greet the dawn.

CHAPTER 6

Jacob jumped from the lowest branch of the tree he had climbed. "We'd best move out quick, Lord Thomas."

"Could you see them?" Johanna asked, as she shoved cooking things into one of the leather packs.

"Nay. Which is good, because it means they cannot see us."

"What a shame," Esther said. "I had hoped we could stay here a day or two."

"We cannot anyway." Thomas straightened from buckling a saddle. "The stream is too far and too shallow. We probably aren't more than a quarter mile from the first tower tree we passed."

Esther tossed a bedroll to him. "That is all—after riding half the day?"

He caught the bedding and strapped it behind the saddle. "We go back and forth more than ahead, and no faster than if we walked." He moved on to ready another horse. "These ponies spare our feet and lighten the load, but they give no speed in this contorted land."

Esther clutched the walking stick he'd smoothed for her and stepped near with barely a limp. "Why do you call them ponies half the time, when they are no such thing?"

He grinned at her. "They seem little to me, but really 'tis because they are bred for rugged packing, not as hunters or riding horses." He gripped her waist. "Up with you, now."

He lifted her to the saddle to spare her mounting with a bad foot. She swung her leg over and situated her split tunic. She had never found that or those petite trousers amidst his mother's clothes. Jacob's family must have given them to her. A good thing, for a lady's gown was not suited to this life. A man's clothes made the switch easier, but his shirt was white no longer and his jerkin, though plain, seemed too fine for this wilderness. Still, he wished there was a way to make her look like the lady she now was. At least she had a gold ring with a pair of dainty sapphires embedded in it.

Thomas mounted and took the rear position, for Jacob was already heading out along a path he'd chosen. They traveled two more days, stopping when they found water. Finding both a stream and a sheltered campsite in the same place seemed impossible, but at least they got better at judging where the land lay easier.

The second afternoon, Jacob dismounted and looked over the ground beneath a maple with vast spreading limbs. "We can rig a tent from this branch for two of us, and that great, tilted rock there is almost as good as a roof for you and your lady. The stream isn't that far, and we just watered the horses. What think you, Lord Thomas, of staying here tomorrow?"

Were they far enough in? They had heard no other folk. 'Twas unlikely that they had covered many miles, but any who entered this wilderness would face the same obstacles. "Aye, two nights and a day at least. That will give us time to rest the horses and scout around a bit."

By the looks on the faces of Esther and Johanna, that plan met their full approval.

Thomas helped Esther from the saddle. "You look relieved, my lady." She still gave an awkward smile when anyone called her that.

"Indeed, I am. Two nights in one place and time enough to make a bed. Could you cut down a pile of those ferns for me?"

The men found places where the horses could reach adequate food, then hunted and brought home a few squirrels and a chubby goat. Or so Thomas thought until he picked it up. More wool than he'd expected.

They returned to an actual camp. Several armloads of wood were stacked beside rocks. Roots and herbs waited beside the cooking pot, and a thick pad of ferns lay ready for night.

Johanna sank her fingers into the wool. "Ooh, be careful with this pelt when you skin the goat." She started the fire, and Esther cleaned roots, while they discussed possible uses for the goat pelt, how best to cook dinner, and several other topics that seemed to sprout from nothing.

Thomas and Jacob moved on to the next tasks, much like on a hunting trip, but work paused when the sun sank low. Thomas leaned back against a log, his belly pleasantly sated, friends near, and Esther's hand in his. Calm crept near and lingered for the first time since the night the village burned. Perhaps because he had a fair bride to rest his gaze upon. She had donned the finest of the gowns she'd brought and a mother-of-pearl bracelet, which he'd inherited from his mother. Simple, compared to court styles, but oh, she looked lovely!

They stayed in this camp a few days. Thomas and Esther shared many a smile over the way Jacob and Johanna kept arranging to give them time alone.

Then the wind grew fitful, and rain poured through the night.

By morn, mud sucked at Thomas's boots, and water stood in every footprint as he and Jacob wrestled the wet canvas into a form they could tie to a pony. Jacob scowled at the slopes surrounding them. "Why didn't we realize this was low ground?"

"Desperate, I suppose. Needing some place to *be*."

They had a miserable time packing, but at least their daily scouting trips gave them more certainty when they set off again.

Mist hid the tops of the tower trees as they trudged through the dripping forest. A ravine proved troublesome, but they spotted a promising campsite on the far side, so they pressed on and found a crossing as drizzle turned to rain.

They got the women across first, then led five ponies up the bank to them. The sixth, they lost, for it stumbled on the wet rocks.

Another awful struggle, first trying to help the pony, then discovering its leg was truly broken, and finally putting it out of its misery. By the time they got the pack cut loose and dragged up the slope, the gray sky was dark. They could do nothing more than huddle in the scant overhang the women had found, chew some dried meat, and wait for the dawn.

Thomas's thoughts sank into a pit darker than the night. He'd led them into such a mess. He'd thought he knew how to live in the woods. Obviously false, and he was no better as a nobleman. He should be leading, deciding, providing the means to accomplish things. Instead, he slumped in the rain, and couldn't even figure out how to apologize.

He could tell from the shifting that no one slept. Were they as worried as he was about how they were going to survive? "How much food is left?" he asked at last.

"We have more horsemeat than we can eat," Jacob said. "We'll get it in the morning. Don't fret, and you might be able to doze."

Dawn proved Jacob wrong. Scavengers had found the carcass.

The men harvested a couple ravens that paused within an arrow's range to eat scraps of horse flesh. 'Twas too wet to cook the birds, so they loaded up and trudged on. The women rode, but both Thomas and Jacob refused to mount the one horse that carried no pack.

The sun fought through the mist when it reached its zenith, and soon after, they found a cave in a hillside, with a stream gurgling below.

They all stared this way and that.

"This looks like a good spot," Thomas said, "but so we thought at the meadow. Let's find the flaws before we decide."

Jacob poked about inside the cave. "There's some dry dung in there, but nothing has visited in months."

"There are a few spots here that are nigh level," Esther said. "I suppose we could wish for an ordinary tree a little nearer, but if that is my worst complaint, this is a fine spot indeed."

Johanna stepped down the rocks at the cave entrance, resting a hand against the overhanging roof. "This lip extends far enough that it kept the interior dry in all that downpour."

"Right, then," Thomas said. "Let's make camp." Pretending he was a leader.

Esther and Johanna took the dry items that were wrapped in oiled leather and stored them in the cave, then spread everything else on roots and rocks.

So many tasks. Arranging a useful firepit. Situating some logs where they could dry the saddles. Tying the horses where they could eat. More hunting.

Johanna cleaned the ravens and carefully stored the primary feathers. She roasted the meat and boiled the rest for soup while Esther found edible plants in the soil between the massive roots of two tower trees. They seemed to hold the hill together.

Thomas kept an eye to her, though she'd already made it clear that she didn't appreciate hovering. When he saw how awkwardly she descended the hillside with her laden basket, he climbed to her. "Why don't you have your walking stick?"

She let out a rueful huff. "'Tis easy to go up just a step here and there, and I need both hands to gather. So I left it, not realizing it would be this hard coming down." She let him lift her over a bad spot. "But you are here now, and that is better anyway."

He tried to smile at the sweetness in her voice, but it didn't work.

As they neared the cave, she asked, "What is wrong, Thomas?"

What sort of question was that? "Everything is wrong. Why do you even ask?"

She sighed. "The only thing that is truly wrong is the way you are looking at all of this. I don't blame you. I know you've lost more than the rest of us. This is no castle, like you have always known. But look at all the things that are right." She drew him into the cave where Jacob was shoveling out the last of the dry dung. "See here on this ledge. All of the maps and papers are dry as a bone, the holy book included, which makes me especially happy. My needles and sheers didn't get wet either."

By the pitch of her voice, that must matter a lot. Rust, perhaps.

"We still have all of our supplies," Esther said, "and though I know you feel bad about the poor pony, we still have five, which is enough. In fact, we are rich compared to most people. We have a dry refuge for the next time it rains." She swept a hand to encompass the cave as she turned him to face outward. "We have an enormous, lovely land to draw sustenance from. Maybe best of all, we have two friends to share it with." Jacob and Johanna returned the smile that sounded in Esther's voice. "Should one of us falter, like I have with my twisted ankle, then another can bear the burden, like you did for me a moment past. So think less of what is wrong, and more of what is right."

Thomas patted her hand, which rested in the crook of his arm. "You are a sweet wife."

"A wise one, too," Jacob said.

Perhaps now Thomas could get an apology out. "You are good friends, as well, for you have fair reason to revile me. You are exiled because of me, and I—"

"For that, I would rather thank you most heartily," Johanna said. "I've always preferred the woods to the castle. What have you in your basket, Lady Esther?"

The women walked off together as Thomas compressed his lips. Jacob clapped a hand on his shoulder and said, "Stop thinking everything is your fault. None of it is, and I'd rather be here with you than in the castle with your brothers. *Far* rather."

Either they were daft, or he was. A less welcome thought... was he moping? If so, that had to stop.

Despite labor-filled days, calm returned to Thomas in the evenings. They settled into a rhythm of lounging together as the sun sank, talking of plans for the morrow, or whatever else occurred. Tonight, Johanna asked for a log free of bark so she could anchor pelts for scraping.

Gazing over the hillside soothed Thomas. There was a subtle quality he liked in the boulders of this hill, the cave, and the majestic tower trees, their trunks as broad as his tower room. Now that the last few days had given him hope that they could survive the summer, he could ponder returning.

CHAPTER 7

Esther squeezed Thomas's hand. "What do you think of, my husband, as you gaze at yon tower tree?"

How sweet to have her at his side—in more ways than one. She had rubbed rosemary through her wet hair, and the long waves hung loose to dry as they sat around the fading fire. He stroked his thumb along the back of her fingers. "I think of towers, not trees. I wonder what has happened at home, and how we will get news. I don't plan to wait on Rufin finding us."

"I grant," Jacob said, "'tis not wise to place any trust in a smuggler, but it is too soon to think of going back."

"Certain. I'm thinking more about whether we have gone deep enough. I also wonder who we heard that morning, and what became of them."

Esther's grip tightened. "You don't mean we have to leave, do you? That is, we're just starting to settle and..."

"Worry not, my lady wife." He rested his free hand over hers, cradling it protectively. "I didn't say we were leaving. 'Tis simply wise to know what goes on elsewhere. If we do need to move, I'd rather have time to pack up and have a route planned."

It took her some minutes to relax as she watched the coals

shrink. He would need to be more thoughtful how he spoke of such matters. Or perhaps he need not speak of them at all. He had already found vantage points around the hill where he could make use of his long vision to scan every approach.

~

THE NEXT MORN, Jacob watched Thomas check southward. "I thought you were looking for prey before, but you're looking for people, aren't you?"

"Both." Seeing neither, he slid down from the rock where he'd perched and continued around, Jacob following.

"What do you fear?" Jacob asked.

"I don't exactly fear anything. I only wish to know if there is something we *should* fear, or if we should just enjoy a summer of hunting." They climbed a rocky piece to higher ground, then walked side-by-side. "I keep thinking about something my father said the day he sent me into hiding. That he didn't know when, or *if*, he would see me again."

Jacob made a sound in his throat. "I can see why that would echo."

"Aye." Thomas braced a foot against a rock and angled his torso. "I wish I knew what King Carleeton—" He hushed his voice and pointed. "Two goats on that log—do you see?"

Jacob dropped to one knee a couple yards to his side. "I'll take the one on the right, you take the left, on count of three." They drew their bows as Jacob counted, then let fly.

Both arrows found their marks in a single goat, and two other goats darted down the trunk and out of sight.

"That was..." Jacob snorted, but Thomas laughed.

"There were three. We both missed the left and right but hit the middle one. First time we got a meal by both of us missing our targets."

Jacob grumbled about impossible lines of sight while they

fought their way through undergrowth to retrieve the goat, which had fallen from the log. Not easily found, but they were determined.

Jacob got their kill ready to carry, while Thomas scrutinized their surroundings. There was something strange... He parted branches and sucked in a breath. "Look!"

Jacob jumped up, then stared.

A dim passage opened before them, roofed by a fallen tower tree. "From above, I thought this trunk rested on the forest floor. 'Tis *yards* above it." For a long moment, they stared. "I have got to know where this leads...*and* how to get the horses down here."

'TWAS PAST NOON when they finally returned to their camp and Jacob could heave the goat from his shoulders.

Esther gave Thomas an unreadable look. "Where have you *been?*"

With his broadest smile, he announced, "We found the perfect trail and just had to follow it."

"Oh, did you now? And leave us wondering if you were lost, or if a bear got you, or who knows what."

He swallowed. "A bear? Why would...we had our bows."

Johanna gripped the cold end of a stout smoldering stick. She threw it back into the fire. "Well, we don't."

By now, he'd taken in that their fire was well stoked for no use, and that extra wood stood ready to light in front of the cave.

"There was a bear?" Jacob spun, bringing bow to hand and drawing an arrow. "Where?"

"We haven't seen it in an hour or two, but it was off beyond the stream." Johanna waved toward a broad area. "I'll not deny it scared us, but we built the fire up, which it must not have liked, though it waved its snout our way plenty before it left. We readied the spears, too, and wood for another fire in case we had to hold out in the cave."

Thomas wrapped an arm around Esther. "Pray forgive me. I'll not leave you again."

She leaned against his chest. "Ah, but you must if you're going to hunt. I shouldn't have harped at you, but I started to worry so, and we could not think even which way we would go if we had to look for you."

"Nay, never wander about looking for us." That thought terrified him far more than a bear approaching their camp.

"How big was it?" Jacob asked.

"Not so big," Johanna said. "Probably a she-bear or young male, with a fine black coat. No cubs."

Esther looked up at Thomas. "We thought about shouting for you, but what you said last night had me scared to do that too."

"I'm glad you both kept your wits," Thomas said. "We're going to have to figure out some whistles. They carry better than words, and maybe we can make them sound bird-like." He scanned the camp, empty of belongings except for the horses' tack. "Did you move everything into the cave?"

"Aye. We've decided to store things packed. We have to take better care of the food anyway." Esther glowered. "Last night, some creature raided all the fresh roots and greens I had gathered and chewed my basket too."

Thomas's elation over the hidden pathway seeped away. Every scrap of good they discovered seemed to be followed by a calamity, whether large or small. At least he was getting more used to it. "I will guard you as you gather more."

When that was done, he and Jacob stayed near but kept to the perimeter, watching for the bear. Such beasts were usually solitary, but even one could be a problem. They hooked waist quivers filled with barbed arrows to their belts, and Thomas carried one of their spears.

"We cannot be standing guard like this every day," Thomas

said. "I've hunted bear before, but with my brothers and some trackers."

"Two of us should be able to bring it down, though I—"

Thomas gripped Jacob's arm and nodded in the direction of a shuffling sound. He hefted his spear while Jacob raised his bow. Something was beyond the green shroud of underbrush. South, more or less, along the game trail that had led them here. Deer would be nice, but this thing made too much noise for that.

He studied the sound a moment longer, then whispered, "'Tis people."

Another minute, and a man pushed through the gap in a stand of giant ferns. He halted, his eyes widening at the arrow and spear trained on him. "We mean no harm," he croaked.

"Who is with you?" Thomas whispered.

"My...my wife. Just us two, my lord."

Thomas recognized him, for the old man wore his hunting jerkin, now with a shirt beneath it. "Best not to be wandering these parts unarmed. A bear came through here this morn."

A wrinkled face peered at them from around the man's shoulder.

"Come up to our camp," Thomas said. He led the way, hoping this wasn't a mistake. A glance over his shoulder confirmed that Jacob had the sense to take a look down that trail.

Esther took one glance at them and exclaimed, "Saul! Ruthie!" 'Twas little surprise that she knew them and swiftly put them at ease.

The woman lowered herself to a log with the aid of her walking stick and groaned before the weight left her knees. She'd acquired more clothing since Thomas saw her last. Trousers too big for her showed below the shortened hem of her night dress. A grassy, woven bundle hung from her shoulder. She said barely a word, but Saul made up for it.

"'Tis good to see you made it out, Esther," he said.

"*Lady* Esther," Thomas corrected. "We joined hands before the priest on the day we left the castle."

"Did you now?"

'Twas more exclamation than question, but Esther said, "Aye." She smiled up at Thomas from her place by the fire, where she tended meat that roasted on sticks.

"That was quite a night," Saul said. "Also the *final* night for some of the Eberle men-at-arms, for the Kaituer castle men know the woods and how to move silently."

"What know you of it?"

"Ruthie and me headed back, thinking we'd have to take refuge at the castle or starve. In the dusk, we saw one of the Eberle men awatchin' the castle, so we hunkered down to wait out the night. He never looked back at all. I saw the form of a man in the dark set upon him from behind. 'Twas over in seconds. The victor bent over him quick, then ran off."

Saul rubbed his nose. "I crept near to see what was what. The Eberle fellow was dead, sure enough, and his quiver and belt sheath empty. We took his clothes and things, plus I found a knife in his boot." He gestured to their haphazard clothing. "That's how we got enough to wear. The bow and quiver are useless till I can make some arrows, but by then, we knew we couldn't stay near the castle. We snuck a little farther into the woods, and after a while, I heard what sounded like a train of smuggler ponies. The next morn, I met some folk who had snuck out of the castle the day before and heard what was going on with the Eberle's. They say your brothers snatched Lady Eberle and—"

"Aye, that much, I know," Thomas said. "Have you any news more recent? Do you know if King Carleeton has come?"

"He's come, all right, with an army! Prince Maerton too. They say he was off to rally the noble houses of Kaituer Duchy against the duke."

His father would be livid if his own nobles turned on him. Holed up within his own castle and no help from the outside—

they wouldn't survive a siege. Not if the local nobles joined the king and his brother. And though Prince Maerton was as inflexible as the king, he had a smooth, persuasive tongue.

Saul was still talking, telling of all the folk who were fleeing into the woods, how it came to be known that the ponies had traveled northwest to enter Tower Woods, and that more folk came with fresh news. The king's army was swelling with local folk, and the smugglers stationed along the route to the sea had fled into the woods.

Awful tidings. "What news have you of the king's doings at the castle?"

"Ah, that's what I'm getting to—and why I came to find you. The king demanded Lady Eberle's release and that all four of the duke's sons be surrendered to him to stand trial for killing the villagers who died in the fire."

Thomas grew stone cold.

Esther had words, of course. "Lord Thomas had nothing to do with that fire, nor anything that went before!"

"Does the king know that?" Saul asked.

Chills raced through Thomas's arms, as silence made the answer obvious.

Saul resumed his tale. "From what I hear, Duke Kaituer stood upon the wall and defied the king, threatening Lady Eberle's life if any moved against him. So the king declared the sons guilty, since they refused trial, and sentenced them to be hanged." Saul looked pained as he met Thomas's eyes, but forged on. "There was a fellow listening to this story in the woods, and he asked if the king knew that Lord Thomas was not in the castle."

"And?" Esther demanded in the silence.

"The one who told the tale said he didn't know. The duke had declared, 'No son of mine shall hang.' He didn't say a number. After that, I thought through all I'd heard, and put that together with the ponies heading northwest. We know you're nothing like your half-brothers from the duke's first wife, so I wanted to warn you. That's why we set out to follow you, even though 'tis not easy on my Ruthie, 'cause she's got the arthritis in her knees."

Johanna had been quietly tending to the goat while they talked, but at that, she straightened and went to the latest batch of greens.

"Nay! 'Tis not right!" Esther jumped up and gripped Thomas's arm. "We are witnesses that you didn't take part—"

He put a finger to her lips. "I know, my dear one, but not just now." An uncanny feeling grew...like he watched all this from far away. Maybe he needed to keep it that way. Though he held his beloved's hand, he turned to Saul. "You followed me on purpose. Was it that easy to track us?"

"Well, a good number of people have gone into Tower Woods now, so there's a beaten path through a wee valley and under a mighty trunk. Probably other ways, too, but that'un's the most used. Nigh everyone stays by the edge, but I traced back and forth while Ruthie rested. Horses leave dung, so I found your trail. We slipped away without telling anyone. If you were trying to cover your trail, you've a lot to learn of that. Besides, there are horse remains in a ravine."

Johanna squatted near the fire and ladled hot broth into a mug of herbs. "We weren't trying to hide it, for we didn't know all this." She handed the mug to Ruthie. "This may help your knees."

"My thanks for your kindness."

Johanna took up the meat that Esther had abandoned. "These are well roasted. Let us eat before we think more on what's to be done."

Thomas drew Esther to sit on a log, which meant that he had to sit also, for she clung to him. Sick though he felt, he needed to soothe her. Johanna served them, which they hadn't bothered with before, but 'twas a good thing, for Esther didn't reach for her portion.

"Split the food six ways," Thomas said.

Saul swallowed, looking at it. "We did not come to leech off of you."

"You brought me news I had need of and deserve a meal for your troubles."

They accepted their portions and wasted no time on the first bite. "I can still hunt," Saul said. "I look ancient, but I'm spry. I'll find me some wood for arrows, for I've always made my own."

"Then teach me how," Jacob said, "and I'll trade food for the skill."

Jacob must have realized the same thing as Thomas. They wouldn't be going back soon. Ever?

They ate in silence, Thomas trying to grasp the fact that he'd been condemned to hang. It just couldn't be. Yet everyone knew —King Carleeton didn't back off his word.

The food was gone before his stomach was filled, and they drank the broth as well.

Esther finally turned her jerky movements into words. "'Tis not just. You have a right to a fair trial, and we are witnesses that you were not part of it. Perhaps if you return now and reason with the king...?"

He rested a hand on her knee. "The only chance of that working was if I had gone to the king before he reached the castle. I am already a fugitive, as condemned by my absence as my brothers are by hiding within the walls."

Ruthie uncoiled her bundle—a half-finished mat—and began weaving long grasses at the rough edge. "Mayhap things will settle, in time," she said. "Once the king cannot find you in the castle, he may learn from local folk that you were not in league with your brothers."

He wanted to grasp at that straw. Flimsy hope. Too many classed him with his brothers. The Kaituers were a tight-knit clan, true enough. The villagers had not seen him light the fire, but what of it? They hadn't seen him asleep in his bed either. For that matter, neither had Esther nor Jacob. He had no witness of innocence. Would the king even care if some thought better of him? Saul and Ruthie must, and Thomas didn't even know them. Had the gift of a jerkin and maybe a little aid to a destitute mother swayed them? How many others would speak for him? He could not test this. If the king captured him now, he might use Thomas as a hostage to force the duke's hand. Which his father would deem the ultimate betrayal.

"In any case," Thomas said, "I cannot go back now. Until the king discovers that I am not at the castle, he will not search farther, so we have time to consider."

CHAPTER 8

The dawn brought them a bear. A rude awakening, but they triumphed. Thomas and Jacob stood panting over the dead beast, once they were sure they had killed it.

"This kind of excitement," Jacob said, "is not how I like to start the day."

"Gets the juices flowing, it does." Saul still held his bow half-drawn.

"Think of all the hunting time it has saved us." Thomas took a last scan around the hillside opposite their camp. "I'm going to fetch a pony and tell the women all is well." He jumped the stream, delivered the welcome news, and returned with a horse to carry their bounty. "Johanna is thrilled. She said not to spoil the pelt."

Jacob looked up from his labor. "Johanna *always* says not to spoil the pelt."

"One would think she is the tanner's daughter," Thomas said with a grin. "A bearskin will improve the cave floor, and Ruthie spoke of making glue."

After breakfast, they found a space between boulders where they could hang meat and keep a fire burning slow beneath it. Better yet, it was near a couple of the south vantage points. Or was that a bad thing? Thomas couldn't help but watch the approaches between feeding the fire.

Saul told them which wood made the best arrows and began teaching Jacob how to prepare the shafts.

Jacob cast many glances at Thomas and finally asked, "You are not expecting the king's men already, are you?"

"Nay."

"Speak your mind, then, for you look south too often."

"Saul said that smugglers have taken refuge in Tower Woods."

Saul nodded, sighting down the length of the shaft he worked on.

Jacob turned the corners of his mouth down. "Hmm. That is not good."

"'Tis not. There are too many ways they can make mischief. Also, our trail is easily followed."

"We will be more careful."

"Aye, but that only matters when we are moving."

"You are thinking of heading north again?"

"We must. And…" Thomas looked at Saul. "We must also make it look like we were not here. As though the trail leads to… someone else. Someone whom neither the smugglers nor the king would care about."

Saul's fingers stilled on the shaft. "Me and Ruthie?"

Thomas nodded. "If you are willing. You would gain a fair camp, part of the bear meat, and a pony."

"You'd leave one of your horses?"

"Aye. For a horse trail leads here."

"A horse trail—*of four*—will also lead away."

"There is a hidden route that we can take. If you simply obscure our passage out of the camp, we will be difficult to find. When we have settled, one of us will come back to show you the route, or at least hear whether you have news. If you care to brave the journey, you could bring me word, perhaps in early autumn, of...what happened at the castle." Still his chest ached too much to frame words around his true fear.

Saul smoothed the shaft.

"Think on it," Thomas said. "I need to talk with Lady Esther. I will send Ruthie here so you can mull things over."

Esther had no liking for it but accepted the need to move on. Johanna merely listed some preparations and began carrying water from the stream to wash clothes.

Thomas cradled Esther's hand, wishing he could do so much more for her. "You may have all of tomorrow to gather and prepare for the journey."

She sighed. "I'd best show Ruthie, or maybe Saul, where the herbs grow in that sunny patch."

He caught the hint of what she really meant and remembered how happy she had been to find sun-loving herbs. A lady of the House of Kaituer...so impoverished that she mourned the loss of herbs.

"I'll claim we found two horses wandering in the woods," Saul said as they sat by the cooking fire, "and lost one in the ravine. If they recognized that more horses traveled together, I can say I followed your trail for a time but lost it."

Thomas nodded. Not perfect, but the best explanation so far. They kept at it, figuring out how to make every detail of the camp plausible. They would have to leave a couple barbed arrows to explain the bear kill, for neither he nor Jacob could part with a spear. Saul needed the arrows, anyway. Johanna had already found a sharp rock that Ruthie could use to scrape the bearskin. It seemed that they were sharing so little with the elderly couple who would need to survive on their own, but Saul and Ruthie kept acting like they were generous.

ONE LAST NIGHT in the safety of the cave, then they packed up and set off. Saul followed them through underbrush to the beginning of the hidden way they had found where the woolly goat fell. He would backtrack and ensure no sign remained of their passage.

"Don't be worrying so much about Ruthie and me," Saul said at parting. "Likely, some other villagers will come upon us. Fare you well now."

They traveled in silence, Thomas leading with a pack-laden pony, the women on their mounts, and Jacob following the fourth horse to check and obscure the trail if need be. The hidden way felt like a tunnel, with the fallen tower tree as a roof. No sunlight reached the ground, which was more rock than soil. Beyond that covering, ferns made a wall on the left and all manner of bushes shielded their right side. Even when they wove from beneath the trunk, the turned-up roots formed another wall, sprouting plants of its own. Animals must have kept the ferns at bay, for a narrower path continued and soon another root formation turned the path north again.

On they traveled, seemingly through a lower forest beneath Tower Woods, until at last the land sloped upward toward an odd tree. Its peeling bark revealed mottled orange wood. This ended the stretch that Thomas and Jacob had scouted. Now, they were back to climbing trees for a view or short treks of scouting. By late afternoon, they found a patch surprisingly like a meadow, with a few aspens dwarfed by the tower trees. How welcome to have room for two tents! The horses happily set to grazing.

"This is a strange woodland," Johanna said, staring around the varied landscape.

Esther dismounted. "Aye, but bounteous too. Let's get the cook pack out."

Her hopeful peace always soothed Thomas. He could not have found a better wife anywhere. A noble lady would have floundered terribly in this wilderness, but although Esther directed their camp like it was her little manor house, she also worked alongside Johanna. Thomas smiled and went to help Jacob hobble the horses.

Their journey was methodical now. Scout, move on, and camp each evening. At times, they found more hidden ways, caves, and even a tunnel a few hundred yards long beneath a vast leaning boulder. Once, Thomas and Jacob got so lost while hunting, they never would have found the women were it not for the whistles they had practiced. Finally, they reached the River Vale.

Thomas had known they would, for it flowed northwest from the city of Purthellia, but exactly where it cut its channel was a mystery...until now. He and Jacob stood looking down a cliff face, perhaps twenty feet to the frothing river. They would not be fording it. Even near the city, a bridge was needed to cross it.

"I hope we've traveled far enough," Jacob said.

"Likely so. Let us scout thoroughly for a permanent site."

A tower tree lying across the river caught Thomas's attention. "'Tis an old one," he said, climbing onto it. He rapped his boot heel against a remnant of the heartwood. "Solid, though I think it must have broken off yon rotting stump." He walked a little farther between the aged, cracked wood that formed walls taller than him. He stopped where the crevice grew too narrow to pass. By sound and distance, he must be halfway across the river. Turning back, he said, "Let's fetch the women and gear, and make ourselves a home near here."

There were several caves to choose from. They found two, not far separated, above a stream. Thomas watched Esther's face. "What think you of this site? Could you settle here?"

Her blue eyes half closed as her smile bloomed. "Ah...*settle!* What a beautiful word. Aye, a two-room house with a vast garden."

"You, my lady wife, are lovely inside and out." He kissed only her fingers, for Jacob and Johanna were watching.

Day followed day as they settled into the business of living.

Esther made a habit, now, of sitting with a mug of pine needle tea and reading by the light of the rising sun before she joined Johanna in whatever needed doing.

Today, Esther closed the holy book and asked, "Was the moon full last night?"

"I believe so," Thomas said. "Why?"

"My grandmother used to keep the rest days, and I just read the piece about it. That we and our beasts are to rest the day after the full moon, new moon, and each half moon. It says, 'Lest our health fail and our hearts grow weary in labor, we must take a day to rejoice and rest in the favor of our God.'" She smiled as only she could. "What think you, my husband?"

He couldn't help but return her smile. Somehow, these words called to him. Perhaps because his mother used to read to him from that book. Though life had gone all wrong, this moment held a hint of peace. "What can I say, but to agree with my lady wife. My mother kept the rest days, too, so you follow her in wise management of our household."

Unfortunate that this rest day gave him more time to wonder what had become of his home...his family. Jacob had gone back after they settled here, insisting that he would be safe enough alone. Indeed, he had returned swiftly, aided by the hidden ways they had followed here. A few other homeless villagers now gathered at their former camp, though they had nothing new to tell. A smuggler had passed through, searching for Lord Thomas, but Saul had revealed nothing. Jacob had shown him more of the route northward before returning.

Thus, it was not a total surprise when Saul arrived, leading a bedraggled caravan.

CHAPTER 9

S aul looked so worn down that Thomas held his questions until Esther had given him a mug of broth to drink by the fire.

Jacob went to see that the others sat down to rest for a time, then returned, bringing a man of about thirty with wide-set eyes. "Lord Thomas, this is Miles."

He bowed. "I have wanted, this past month, to thank you for your kindness to my wife, Sarah, and our children." Thomas's confusion must have shown, for Miles said, "You gave her a goat to feed them before I was able to find them in the woods."

"Ah." Thomas sought words. "I'm glad it helped, though 'twas meager."

Miles tilted his head. "I don't know that, but it gave her hope. Also, a basket for our babe so she could rest her weary arms. She worried that she'd sounded ungrateful, but she was exhausted and afearing I was dead."

"Understandable."

Jacob frowned as he waited through this exchange. "Saul, I didn't see Ruthie with the others. Where is she?"

He drew a long breath. "Gone on to our maker, she has."

What? Thomas's throat closed like it always did at the wrong times. He stood a bit behind Saul, so he gripped the man's shoulder while Lady Esther murmured condolences. So much grief.

Saul nodded. "I reckon her knees don't hurt no more, but 'tis mighty hard to forgive those cursed smugglers."

"What happened?" The dip in Thomas's voice surprised even him.

"Rufin's leading that foul gang now. They've been searching for you, and after a while, they wouldn't believe none of us knew where you were." Saul scowled. "I wouldn't tell the likes of him whether the sun had risen! He took the cave for his own, including what little we had inside it, and claimed your horse too." Saul clenched his fist and rocked on the log like he was going to leap up and punch the absent Rufin. "Nothing for us to do but to sneak away in the night."

Thomas looked to the valley, his stomach knotting. "With all of them?"

"Nay, my lord," Miles said. "Just my family and a few others. Already, we knew there would be trouble, for a dozen smugglers were with Rufin, eyeing the women and demanding our food. We did our best to cover the hidden way and then traveled for a day. Ruthie nigh collapsed onto her mat that eve, all soaked in sweat and rubbing her chest. She was gone, come morn. They did not kill her outright, but certain the journey and fear did. We left the hidden way to bury her, and it was that day that we happened upon the first of this group. We found others here and there, all trying to figure out how to survive. Once we reached the River Vale, we followed it westward."

No surprise in any of that. There was only so much land between Kaituer Duchy and the River Vale. Not much farther west of here, they would find the cliff where the river plummeted to the sea. Thomas had seen it from a fishing boat once, with the tower trees atop the cliff. *Before* he knew what those fishing boats were used for at night.

"We didn't mean to lead smugglers to you," Saul said. "They aren't following us—yet anyway."

"I cannot hide forever. I just need to stay away from the king until he's ready to listen to my side of the story. Do you have any news yet from Kaituer Castle?"

By the looks on their faces, he knew it would be bad, but even still, Miles's grim statement of, "It has fallen," didn't register.

"What has fallen?" Esther asked.

"Both the castle and the House of Kaituer."

Esther edged nearer to Thomas and entwined her fingers with his. He stared at the ground for a long moment. "Tell me what you know."

"The nobles all turned on your father, save only your mother's family, the House of Navayn, which wanted the king to exempt you from his verdict. There's all manner of talk of siege craft that the king brought or was constructing. The duke had no hope of withstanding, so your brothers brought Lady Eberle onto the wall. Threatening her life, the duke demanded that the king withdraw. They did not account for the lady having a warrior's heart. She shouted out, 'Do not yield,' and 'Carve my monument from the stone of these walls.'"

Miles clenched the hem of his stained jerkin. "The army must have had a trebuchet ready, because they hurled a great stone at the wall. Then, your brothers picked Lady Eberle up and threw her from the parapet."

Esther and Johanna gasped, but Thomas couldn't breathe. How could they be such beasts? Such crass fools?

"Almost worse than that," Miles said, "she didn't die right away. Her men-at-arms couldn't reach her beneath the archers until they got a covering assembled. Then, they carried her away from the wall. 'Tis said she died hours later."

'Twas all Thomas could do to get air through his lungs.

"In the end, the king breached the walls and the keep. The duke and his sons locked themselves within a room beyond the hall. When that was finally breached, the Kaituers fought to the death. Both the king and prince led the fray, with a score of the king's men and local men too. 'Tis said that the duke fell last, threatening that Lord Thomas and his heirs would hunt the House of Fraetinloch forever."

Thomas could bear no more. He turned and strode from camp to the cliff over the River Vale. His chest and throat ached. Fists clenched. Breath heaving. The frothing waters below were tame compared to his unspeakable rage. He battled the fury pounding through him. Such loathing that he pulled the Kaituer dagger from its sheath on his belt and raised it to fling it into the river. Something deep within stopped his defiant gesture. He could not throw his name—his self—away. Besides, he had a wife to defend. Friends...though why they didn't hate him... He ground his teeth.

Esther and Jacob had followed him. Jacob stood watchful along the cliff edge, but Esther came right up to him and swept her fingertips down his left arm. "I am here," she said.

The reminder he needed...that there was good somewhere in the world, though evil pursued him. He knew not how long he stood trying to subdue the tumult in his soul.

Finally, Esther gave his arm a tiny tug. "Please, Thomas, will you come and sit with me?"

She sounded worried. He shouldn't leave her like that. They found a rock to perch on, side by side, and Jacob left them alone. She tucked her hand within the crook of his arm, like she was going to hang onto him no matter how long he fought the current of his rage.

At length, Thomas managed words. "I know the holy book says we aren't supposed to hate." Another breath. "But I hate them all right now. The king and the prince. The Eberles. My idiot brothers. And my father...the one who should have at least *tried* to clear me...he just spiked their lust for vengeance hotter than it was before. And—" He bit the words off. That they endangered his beloved Esther too. True...and more unforgivable than all the rest...but he must not say that to her. Not cause her any more fear than she already felt.

"Hate them for a day if you like, Thomas. Then, remember they are blind and turn your hatred against evil." She rose, positioned herself between his knees, and put her cool hands against his cheeks. He couldn't help but lift his eyes to hers. "*Especially* remember... I...love...you."

He wrapped his arms around her and drew her close. 'Twas said that love was stronger than hatred. Now, he believed it.

WHEN THE FIRE in his mind had cooled enough for reason, they returned to the newcomers. Thomas stood with Jacob, looking over the clustered families beside the stream.

Miles saw him and strode up the slope, with Saul following. "Everyone is wondering about...well, everything. Where to sleep, where to find food, whether there are bears about..." He scratched his beard. "Even an argument about where to seek privacy."

"Downstream," Thomas and Jacob said in unison.

"Aye, we already solved that one."

"I catch your point," Thomas said. "This is a lot of people close together. We have found enough to eat, but that won't last if we all remain atop one another. Jacob and I know of several caves, for this land is riddled with them. I am thinking that the families with the youngest children should get those, so we can keep the little ones out of the worst weather. Then we will have to see about other shelter."

Miles nodded, looking satisfied.

"Then, we must think of hunting," Thomas said. "How many have bows, how many arrows between them, and..." He turned to Saul. "How fast can we make more?"

Such decisions filled the days, especially as more people arrived, for someone had run back to spread the word. Then, a day came when *many* more arrived. Jacob and Miles insisted that Thomas and Esther stay out of sight at first but soon reported that they were not the king's men.

"I recognize friends among them," Miles said. "They were from our village and went to Eberle manor after the fire."

Thomas raised his brows.

"The House of Eberle thought they would get the duchy, but the king proposed to make Prince Maerton a royal duke, and the Assembly of Duchies voted in his favor. The land is now called Maerton Duchy."

Another jab to Thomas's gut, but he'd learned to steel himself when news arrived.

"Lord Eberle..." Miles sneered with that name. "...is sour over not getting what he coveted. He sent all of our villagers away, telling them to seek aid from Duke Maerton. But the new duke is so accursed harsh, and he has men-at-arms riding the near woods to find smugglers. His men shoot first, and when they make a mistake, they leave widows crying with nothing more than, 'I crave your pardon.'"

So much for peace in the duchy. Time to see about settling more folk. Esther came with Thomas now as he met new arrivals. She was good at seeing needs that he missed and figuring out how to settle orphans and lone stragglers. Though many of these folk had known her as the child Esther, they dropped slight curtsies and called her Lady Esther. It did his heart good, but 'twas strange as well, seeing that he was both disinherited and condemned. Yet these folk looked to him for answers.

He pondered that oddity as he sat with Esther, Jacob, and Johanna around their evening fire, drinking pine needle tea.

"Everyone from the oldest to youngest," Jacob said, "knows to run word to us, should anyone approach. All these folk scattered about may give us some warning, true enough, but it worries me that there is just no way to hide you if the king were to send men searching."

"In a way, there never was," Thomas said. "Delay was all we could ever achieve. That is why I wanted our home site near that trunk over the River Vale. 'Tis why we work a little more at it each day."

"'Twill be some time before the cleft channel is wide enough for horses to cross."

"I know. If need be, we could climb up from the heartwood and cross the breast of the log on foot. 'Twould be difficult to get along without our supplies, but we'd escape."

"Have you ever heard the stories from Selta Duchy?" Jacob asked. "They tell of strange beasts and mystical waters north of the river."

"A dozen versions, no two the same." Thomas shrugged it off. "I've heard more fearsome stories of Tower Woods, but we only found rugged terrain and wooly goats. Which, by the way, run to and fro across that trunk. Bears have even crossed it. If there were strange creatures beyond the river, they would also be among us."

Thomas firmed his grip on Esther's hand and smiled at her. "Worry not over any of this, my dear one. The king did not pursue the wanderers who have come, so I don't expect him soon."

He did not say that smugglers worried him more than the king. Too many of the homeless folk who joined him had been harassed or robbed of what little they possessed. 'Twas for this very reason that they now banded together.

Even more than kings and smugglers, Esther worried him. She'd been picking at her food lately but insisting nothing was wrong. The next morning proved she was ill, for she tossed up her breakfast after a few bites.

Thomas went cold. He *could not* loose Esther!

Johanna merely turned a narrowed look upon her and asked, "When was your last menses?"

Esther made an odd quirk with a corner of her mouth. "The week before I wed Lord Thomas."

What did...?

Johanna's placid voice reached a high pitch. "Oh, my, my!"

"What?" Thomas demanded.

Esther leaned near and laid a hand on his knee as she patted her belly. "I think we'll have a child, come spring."

CHAPTER 10

When Rufin finally arrived, the folk making new homes in Tower Woods outnumbered the smugglers with him. Those living nearby conveyed their opinion with drawn bows and shouts of, "Your kind's not welcome here."

Thomas received the news from Miles, then sent him and Jacob to escort only Rufin to a meeting area, from which no home site could be seen.

Perhaps this was a moment when a little show was in order. Thomas donned the only doublet he'd brought on the journey and belted on his sword, which bore the Kaituer emblem. In truth, he wasn't skilled with such a weapon, but he didn't intend to use it. He let the hilt of his ornate dagger show too, then went to confront the man.

Rufin stopped a few yards distant from Thomas, flanked by Jacob and Miles with their bows in hand. His gaze darted over points on Thomas's person, and his mouth drew small and tight.

Was it anger, greed, or uncertainty that made his fingers curl and straighten repeatedly? Thomas waited.

Rufin accorded him a small bow. "Lord Thomas."

"What brings you here, since my father could not have sent you to find me?"

It took him a minute to answer. "I take it you know what's happened, then. That your father and brothers fell to the swords of the king. That makes you the Duke of Kaituer."

"Do not ever call me that!"

Again, Rufin paused. "I didn't think to hear you disown your own house."

"You have not. My name remains, but the title of duke will never be mine. Has not the king and the Assembly of the Duchies created Prince Maerton as the new duke? Does he not now hold Kaituer Castle?"

"Aye, he struts about with a yellow and green sash, but no one will ever hold Kaituer Castle again. They raided everything of value and battered it for day upon day. The wall is utter ruin, and the keep's roof crashed down through the floors. There is no shelter for any who lived nigh it. Maerton heaps vengeance upon us all."

"All?" Thomas let skepticism seep into that word. "Or is it the smugglers who feel his vengeance?"

"Why should we? Because we brought goods up from the merchant vessels?"

"You know well that goods arriving lawfully through Portlen were taxed to defend the whole land of Lavaycia, and that Kaituer Duchy avoided paying their share with your illegal trade."

"We did as ordered by our lawful duke."

Did they? Were *all* of their deeds ordered by the duke? Arguing over the past wouldn't help Thomas. He needed to know what the smugglers planned.

Rufin's narrowed eyes shifted as though he searched for a crack in Thomas's demeanor. "Now his followers would be loyal to you."

"Why would they follow me, when I was the only Kaituer *not* involved with them?"

Rufin sneered, revealing the gaps in his darkened teeth.

"Have you no pride in that name you speak? Will you not avenge your dead?"

"The dead, I can no longer help. Only the living matter now."

"Then lead us. Do not pretend you have no following." Rufin gestured to both sides, for indeed, men had quietly gathered, one by one, ringing the area. "If we all join together, we have a chance against Maerton's men-at-arms. They are not beyond counting. Now that so many of us have suffered from their rampaging through our land, we can ride the changing tide and drive them out. We need you to lead us. Will you not restore to your own people what is rightfully ours?"

Thomas glanced around the faces...read doubt and guarded speculation on them. Could these folk be swayed so easily?

"And you, Lord Thomas," Rufin said, "do you disdain your own inheritance? Maerton now dwells in your mother's home, Navayn Manor, which she bequeathed to you."

Yet another barb of injustice to rouse his anger, but all these words reeked of deception. "Says the man who, even now, preys upon those whom he beckons to join him. 'Tis true that lost comforts are tempting, but shall we join those who brought our house down? Should we trust a lawless gang to raise it up again? Even after its fall, was it not you who robbed my impoverished friend of the arrows he needed for hunting, who drove him from the cave where he and his wife sheltered, and who shortened the life of an aged woman by stealing the horse I left her? You talk as though you would take their part against injustice, but even if we could win, you would shift with the next day's tide, to abuse them again. Nay, I will not lead anyone back into the very thing that brought the king's wrath upon the guilty and innocent alike."

Spittle hovered on Rufin's snarling lips, and he spat on the ground. "Coward!"

"Nay, for a coward fears to face the truth. I shall protect what I have, not grasp after what the king and the Assembly have lawfully granted to another. Though I am innocent, I accept my exile, and I shall not rise against the House of Fraetinloch."

Rufin sneered. "Know that your portrait hangs in the hall of Maerton's dwelling, where all his men can study the face they hunt. Wouldn't it be tragic if the duke discovered where you live?"

"Indeed," Thomas countered, "for the one who sought to betray me would die before he could speak. You come here pretending strength, when in truth, you are too weak to stand on your own. Else you would not have sought to trick us into joining you. Stay away from our new homes, or we will drive you back to Maerton Duchy. I advise you to live from your own efforts, for the woodland can meet your needs if you would hunt instead of thieving. Be off with you now."

Rufin spun around and stomped away. Jacob and Miles dogged his footsteps, and the ring of men flanked them. Just as well.

The roused confidence that had fired his words departed, leaving Thomas oddly deflated. Before the loneliness of this empty gathering place could overtake him, Esther ran to him and flung her arms around his chest.

"You are the best Kaituer to ever draw breath," she said. "Stronger and wiser than all of them put together! Ugh, that sword won't let me hug you proper."

He chuckled, resting his hands on her shoulders, but said, "Didn't I tell you to stay safe in the cave?"

"We stayed safe behind the ferns instead." Esther nodded toward Johanna, who'd followed her from their hiding place. "I wanted to know what was happening, so Johanna came too. Besides, the wife of my fine lord should not cower. You were splendid! I've never heard you say so many words together, and every one of them was perfect."

Others, mostly women, were beginning to approach, so Thomas bowed over her hand and said, "I thank you, my lady wife." Fortunately, that stemmed her enthusing, because it was a bit embarrassing. Still, there was no denying it warmed him.

The men returned from escorting their unwelcome visitor, and they warmed him even more. Not with anything they said. 'Twas their manner. Straighter shoulders. Slight bows when they drew near him. Not all had accorded him that before, and he had made no issue over it. Now, their quiet respect was his. They spoke of keeping a daily watch, without overburdening those farthest out.

Someone said, "I never could understand why the old duke kept in league with those scoundrels."

"Because it saved him paying taxes," Thomas said. "The Kaituers see to their own duchy first, then to the king and the rest of Lavaycia—only if they must. My grandfather never wanted the southern duchies of Othair and Portlen to join Lavaycia, nor did he want an Assembly that could impose laws upon all. When they decreed that all sea trade should come through the Portlen harbor and be taxed, he defied them by smuggling."

"One crime always begets another," Saul said, "so all who dealt in the gang kept getting worse."

True words, most likely. The Kaituers had long provided evidence for them...had now died for ever more heinous crimes.

But not Thomas, so it couldn't be the final truth. Betrayal and loss still nipped him in dark times, but he'd come to wonder if they also freed him. No more must he be loyal to those who would rather see him hunted than cleared. They had cost him his inheritance, but it seemed that he'd gained another.

Now, if he could just keep it. Those words he'd said—that he would not rise against the House of Fraetinloch. They needed to reach the king, not a smuggler. But how?

THE DAYS SETTLED into peaceful labors again. Their four remaining horses now dragged logs or carried heavy game, like the bears that tried to reclaim their wintering caves. Those who borrowed the horses' strength returned them with a cut of meat or a skin. A small cave with a cleft roof became the shared smokehouse of the scattered settlement. One family found a stand of tall grasses that they harvested for fiber. They wove a sort of linen, and Esther had used their thread to sew an infant gown, which she cut from one of her shifts. Others spun wool from the goats. Johanna had found a beehive in a rotting tree, which Jacob felled for her. Honey, soaps, lotions, and even some candles replaced their dwindling supplies or were traded for other needs.

One labor called urgently to Thomas—the bridge over the River Vale. Several of the men perceived the need almost as strongly as he did. Throughout each day, someone was always at work with the saw or ax from Thomas's supplies, widening the cleft in the outer layers of the huge trunk. He and Jacob also scouted extensively, often taking others with them, as they explored the obscured sunken forest and meandering trails. Thomas sketched a map to lay alongside his map of Kaituer Duchy. If they had to flee from the king's men, they would know the routes and hiding places.

Still, he longed to be free of that danger. Esther's belly swelled with their child. She needed a place of safety, with no threat of sudden pursuit, especially as the weather cooled.

Was the absence of news a false lull? From time to time, a few members of the smuggler gang would bring iron tools to trade, but they knew nothing more of happenings in the duchy. Worse, Thomas suspected that the items they traded were stolen. Such a dilemma, for his people desperately needed tools. Those who had fled from the burning village even felt that such goods were owed to them. He understood...but the former owners of stolen iron would not.

He hated to bring it up, especially with Esther near, but it needed to be said. As usual, they gathered on the rest day following the moon's phases. The night's frost melted as they all carried food to their gathering place. While the meal cooked, Esther read aloud from the holy book, which eased those who missed the village church. Then, they shared food and talk. Thomas prompted them to speak of needs that required joint labor. He also let disagreements be aired, provided that the contenders were willing to settle them, not just bicker.

When bellies were satisfied, Thomas said, "Today, I must raise my own concern. Some of you deal with smugglers, and I worry that they bring you stolen goods. Those they robbed would call you thieves if they found their belongings in your hands."

The countering arguments he expected were voiced, until finally someone snapped, "You and yours have tools, Lord Thomas. Why do you deny them to us?"

"Give over now," Saul said. "He has shared aplenty."

Thomas raised his hands to quiet the stir. "I would deny you nothing. Nor can I tell you not to trade. Yet strive to trade honestly. Remember that *dis*honest dealings brought the king's wrath upon even those who did not deserve it. You risk the same when you trade in stolen goods. Enough has been said of this. Let each see to their own deeds." He watched faces, which told him well enough who would heed his warning.

He glanced at Esther, who watched much as he had, her lips tight. By evening, he'd seen the change in their home site. Everything was stored away in bundles again. Accessible, yet ready to load if they must flee. His heart ached, but he acknowledged the truth.

A bit of good news filtered to them, that Duke Maerton and his men were staying within a day's ride of their homes. The duke had chosen a new castle site farther east of the ruins of Kaituer Castle. Would the lengthy construction keep him home? Would this reprieve last?

The families nearest to Thomas in persuasion counseled him

not to trust that. The bridge must be finished. Cold slowed them, but snow rarely fell during the day. Any that clung to branches at dawn soon melted.

At last, they cleared the far end, which meant they must scout again. Thomas returned so late that night, he needed a torch to light his path home. He snuffed it by the firepit, felt his way into the cave, and crawled under the bearskin beside Esther.

"Oh, I'm so glad you are back," she murmured, snuggling against his chest.

His tired muscles released. "I didn't mean to worry you. The far side gave us a rugged start, but we found a route and first campsite."

"Did you find mysterious animals?"

His chest shook. "Not a one, my love."

A WEEK of balmy weather lifted Thomas's spirits...and his fears. Esther looked enormous. How could he take her on a trek into fresh wilderness? How could he keep her here, now that spring allowed Duke Maerton's men to range farther? Several families had decided to join them as they crossed the River Vale and sought permanent homes. Including—to his great relief—a midwife.

Now, he had a constant debate on his hands. The unseen duke on one side. Possible snow without shelter on the other. And a wife who might begin labor at any moment. That last part made him shudder.

A dozen times, or so it seemed, Thomas persuaded Esther that it would be best to cross over and get settled in a new home before she delivered. Always, she agreed, then a few pains would tighten her belly and change her mind. Finally, the midwife convinced her those were false pains and they should all set out. Then, one of the outer families escorted a new couple to the gathering place.

Jacob and Thomas exchanged a scowling look.

"You'd best go see if there's news," Johanna said. "We'll continue packing."

Keeping his voice low as they walked, Jacob said, "I don't care who they are, or what they say, we leave in the morning."

That didn't seem worth answering. They followed the path around a tree and stepped down some roots to the clearing.

Jacob halted and exclaimed, "Kat!"

Jacob's sister? Small wonder he greeted her with joy, for he had assumed his family lost in the castle's fall. Though she smiled, there was strain in her eyes too. What had she endured?

Katherine drew the man who followed her forward. "I married a few months ago. This is my husband, John."

Jacob greeted him but soon asked his sister about their parents. As she murmured the sad tidings, Thomas realized John was studying him.

Miles must have noticed something strange too, for his voice sounded low. "Where are you from?"

John named one of the villages about ten miles east of Kaituer castle. Odd.

"What brings you here?" Miles asked.

"My wife, of course, desperate to know what became of her brother."

She would be. Others were asking of Duke Maerton's men and whether the travelers had encountered any of the old smuggler gang. It seemed that Tower Woods was still quiet. At least that much was good news.

"Come to my home site," Jacob said, turning to lead the way. "I daresay we can find you a bite to eat."

Miles scowled at their backs until they were beyond hearing. "I don't like it."

They had long since agreed that newcomers were never brought near Thomas's home site, which was in view of Jacob's. Yet this was his sister. Her husband, though...whom no one knew.

"I must go to share the evening talk," Thomas said. "Make a round of the outer home sites, and make sure a careful watch is kept and runners are ready to carry word."

"Aye, my lord."

Thomas learned nothing by the fire, save only that Katherine seemed taut and John insisted he would pitch their tent, rather than sleep in the cave with Jacob and Johanna.

Thomas and Jacob looked down the slope to where John strung up their canvas, one end nigh some bushes with fresh, green leaves.

Saul sauntered near. "I hear tell of hastyberry bushes east along the river," he said, then dropped to a whisper. "Moved ponies to the bridge. We pack quiet."

Jacob nodded. "Ah, then I predict every child will offer to pick berries tomorrow."

"Bid them await word," Thomas murmured, then said aloud, "If we hope to get a taste of that treat, best warn the children that berries stain lips. We will know who snitched."

Saul chuckled. "I wager they won't care, but I'll see that they save you some." He strolled away, looking carefree.

Jacob turned to walk back toward his cave. Trouble tugged at his brow. "She's my *sister*."

Thomas gave his shoulder a pat as they walked. "I know." May Jacob be spared the pain of betrayal. May they all be spared it.

THE SETTING SUN gave dim light to his cave, where Esther had waited out of sight. At least for today, there had been no mention of her or the child she carried. Everything was packed and tied, save only the clay pot she needed at night and the bearskin where they slept. So she was worried too.

Thomas sat beside her on the black fur and told her of the

talk. Should he tell her of preparations? Aye, she had better know the possibilities.

"But 'tis Kat," she said, when he finished. "I've known her all my life."

"Mm. She didn't ask about you."

A long silence passed before Esther said, "She must know we married."

"Aye. 'Tis possible her husband doesn't know. 'Tis John that worries me most."

Esther drew a deep breath and let it out. "As though it isn't hard to sleep already!"

He kissed her forehead. "I know, my love, but we had best try."

They settled together, both of them fully dressed, lest they must flee in the night. He had the satisfaction of hearing her breath slow with sleep. If only he could do the same, but words revolved through his mind. 'Twas dark indeed when he heard footsteps outside.

He sat up, reaching for the spear he kept nigh to hand.

A soft whisper reached him. "Lord Thomas, 'tis Jacob. Wake up."

"Enter."

Esther stirred beside him, and a breath of cool air shifted. Faint gray barely silhouetted Jacob as he pushed aside the deerskin over the entrance and pulled someone into the cave with him.

"Who is with you?" Thomas asked.

"Kat! They came to betray us!"

"'Tis not like that," Kat whimpered. "I was going to warn you before it was too late."

Another awful moment to get through. To get Jacob through.

Esther fumbled through one of their packs, then struck a flint and lit their candle. Flickering light revealed tears on Kat's cheeks and Jacob's grip on her wrist.

His voice remained harsh. "One of the watchmen saw

someone leave the camp on the south edge. Heard him, mostly, for he avoided the moonlight. The watchman reported, and Miles brought me word. I checked Kat's tent and found that John was gone."

Kat's tears still flowed. "I was asleep. I would have told you as soon as I knew he'd left."

'Twas hard to understand her, she squeaked so. Thomas stood. "I'll give you a chance to explain, so compose yourself." Taking the candle from Esther, he set it in the crack that best anchored it.

Esther leaned against the cave wall, still half-snuggled in their bed. "I wish I could have welcomed you earlier, Kat. Let her go Jacob, so she may sit on the bearskin."

Katherine knelt where Esther pointed. "'Twas for the best," she said, "that John did not lay eyes on you, Lady Esther. I am so sorry."

She must be younger than Esther, though perhaps her tears and messy braid made it seem so. She tucked her woolen nightdress around her feet as Thomas sat on one of the sawed-off stumps and motioned for Jacob to take the other.

"Tell me now," Thomas said, "what you would have warned us of."

"John is...well, from our duchy, but he joined up with Duke Maerton when he recruited men-at-arms."

Jacob snorted. "How could you wed such a one?"

"What else could I do? So many men have been killed, and destitute women are everywhere. I thought I could at least be safe and fed."

"Indeed. 'Tis not to be wondered at," Esther said with a firm look at Jacob.

Katherine sniffed. "The duke cares for nothing but hunting the old smugglers and..." Her mouth trembled as she turned pleading eyes to Thomas. "...and you."

"I know."

"'Tis awful. He found out that I am sister to your squire, so I *had* to come with them into Tower Woods. Everyone claims they have not seen you, even when the duke has them beaten." She shuddered. "I don't know who thought of it, but John put off his uniform and dressed like a villager. We were supposed to look for my brother, and in that way, find *you*, Lord Thomas. I know that makes me seem like a traitor, but the duke is ready to slaughter everyone in his path until he finds you. And he will. Everyone knows a lot of villagers have settled here. If he can go straight to your cave, then not so many of them will die."

Aye, she had been sore pressed, and for her last words, he could forgive her choice—if she'd had one.

"We were supposed to find you, then sneak away in the night," Katherine said. "These woods scare me, and John knows it. I played it up even more the last couple nights to convince him that I'd scream at every shadow. So he was going to sneak away, and I was supposed to say he broke out in fever during the night and warn everyone to stay away from our tent."

Jacob exhaled a puff of air.

"I know it was a stupid plan, but it didn't need to work for long. The army is not far."

"How far?" Thomas asked.

"I don't know. Far enough to not be spotted. They're spread out in a long line, so you cannot get around them."

"Can John reach them before dawn?"

"Oh, nay! He just wanted to get out of sight before first light. How could anyone travel these woods in the dark? I know the army planned to stay far enough away so that villagers who went out to hunt wouldn't chance upon them."

Relief in that, for there was no way Thomas could lead families over the rough ground on the river's far bank in darkness. "Dawn, then."

"Should I start rousing them now?" Jacob asked.

"Nay. John may still be within range to hear. We need the sun as much as he does."

"What are you going to do?" Katherine asked.

Jacob glared. "Do you really expect us to tell you?"

"Oh, Jacob! Please forgive me. I didn't have any choice."

"Did it occur to you that they will kill all four of us? Lord Thomas, Lady Esther, Johanna, and me?"

"Perhaps vengeance will content you," his sister snapped. "If they figure out all that I have told you, they will kill me too. And believe me, I know how little excuse they need to start slaughtering."

That shaft must have pierced Jacob's anger, for he looked to the cave floor, then mumbled, "I don't want vengeance. Not for you."

"Take her back to the tent, Jacob. Assign a couple men to keep watch outside so she cannot flee, but they are to do her no harm. When the duke comes, Katherine, you will show him this cave. There will be no need to reveal what you have said."

He looked to Jacob again. "When you have seen to her, find Miles and return to me."

CHAPTER 11

They had not many minutes to wait—minutes Thomas filled with urgent thought—before the two men pushed open the flap.

"The woods are still quiet," Miles said. "Might be about an hour until the dawn twilight."

"Everyone is packed," Jacob said, then looked at Esther. "Johanna wants to know how you are faring."

"Not in labor, if that's what she means. I will ride even if it starts. I hope you make peace with your sister, Jacob. We are ready to leave, so nothing she did makes any difference."

Jacob just scowled.

"She could not have stopped the duke's advance," Thomas said, "but what she told us matters greatly."

"I don't see how, except maybe to warn us to leave before sunrise."

"Nay, we cannot do that. She revealed a danger that hadn't occurred to me."

"Not another!" Esther said. "What do you mean?"

"Many families intended to stay here. If they resist the duke, he will kill every one of them. If they resisted on my behalf, I could never forgive myself. I must meet with them." To Jacob and Miles, he said, "At dawn's first light, summon them to the gathering place. All are welcome, but at least the men must come."

In the silence after they departed, he gathered his resolve and told Esther his two options.

She listened, her lips trembling at first, then hardening. "Stop saying there are two options. You know that I will accept only one of them, for someday, he will discover that I carried a child."

"I know that is so, though it makes me feel cowardly to run."

"It often takes more courage to live than to die." She gripped his arm for a moment. "You are a brave man, Thomas Kaituer." She lay back on their bed. "Best write your letter."

Thomas dug in the oiled leather pouch, then laid parchment on one of the stumps, and dipped a quill in ink.

To my liege, Carleeton of Fraetinloch, King of Lavaycia,

Rumors have reached me in Tower Woods, where I, Thomas, have made my home in exile. By far the most disturbing rumor is that the last Duke of Kaituer declared that I would hunt the House of Fraetinloch. His words were false when uttered and always will remain false.

From witnesses, I learned that my brothers sparked an uprising, then lit the fire which burned the village. I do not fault the crown's judgement or execution of them. I believe my father had no part in the fire, but he had condoned lawless acts so long, that he could no longer prevent them. Since he defied his king, his death was also inevitable. I will not avenge those who draw evil upon themselves, and worse, upon the innocent around them. I, too, know this pain, for I have lost all, even though I am innocent of their evil deeds.

Should we ever meet, my liege, I would hope that you would grant me a trial. Yet it seems that in sending me away before you arrived at Kaituer Castle, my father made me appear guilty and brought an undeserved judgment upon me. I acknowledge that the land of my fathers will never be mine, and thus I accept exile. All of Tower Woods lies beyond my former duchy, yet I shall soon cross the River Vale as well, lest anyone suggest that I linger within Lavaycia.

Though I depart, I leave you my oath. I honor you as my king and swear my allegiance to you. I shall never take up arms against the House of Fraetinloch. In witness whereof, I break my sword this day and leave it with this letter to be delivered to you, my king.
    Thomas Kaituer

He dripped a bit of wax from the candle onto the parchment beside his name and pressed his ring into it. 'Twas just the seal of a younger son, with the *K* of his house and a smaller entwined *T*. Hardly visible in the beeswax. He handed the letter to Esther to read, then drew his sword from its scabbard, where it rested on their packs. Thomas wedged the tip into a crevice and tested its flex.

"Does it pain you to break it?" she asked.

He considered for a moment. Odd. "Perhaps a little—for one is not supposed to do such a thing. I'm good with a bow, but never much cared for swords. 'Tis not a deep loss." He pressed the hilt to the floor, and with a snap, it was done. He laid the hilt across a stump, placing the letter beneath it, then picked up the dagger his father had given him. 'Twas embellished with sapphires—a *K* carved deep in the gold pommel. "Strange, but this I cannot part with." Best not to be seen with it, though. He tucked it into the oiled leather pouch.

Esther was struggling to rise from their low bed, so he bent down to lift her. "Ugh," she grunted as she stood. Then she twined her arms around his neck, and he shifted for the sideways kiss that worked better these days. "I love you so, Thomas Kaituer."

His throat tightened as always, but a long tender kiss answered her better than his words ever could.

THE WAIT SEEMED LONG—THOUGH Thomas knew it wasn't—as folk gathered in their meeting place. Sunbeams angled between massive trunks. Esther had insisted on standing at his side. Jacob and Johanna stood at his other side.

When the gathering seemed complete, Thomas addressed them. "You all know that we were about to cross the river, and we will set out within the hour. But last night I learned that the Duke of Maerton has an army nearby. They may even arrive today."

He waited out the murmurs. "In past months, you've taken turns standing guard, but I advise you not to do so today. Duke Maerton now holds lawful authority, and he will not be lenient if you defy him. I'm told he wears a sash of yellow and green. When you see him, I advise that you bow. He will be looking for me. Point him toward my cave. I have left an open letter for him to give to the king. 'Tis my hope that this will satisfy him enough to leave you in peace."

Some began assuring him of their loyalty, and he lifted his hands for quiet. "The respect and honor you have granted me will warm my heart to my final breath. Yet I have no rights as a lord over you. Call me lord no more, nor anything except Thomas. Do not even speak the name of my house, or your life is likely forfeit, with no gain to anyone. Lest Duke Maerton suspect you of supporting the House of Kaituer, tell him that you gathered here for safety because I would not tolerate smugglers. Let him know that you stand against that gang. 'Tis important that you ally yourselves with him, for he has been extremely harsh. I believe this is the only way you may dwell in peace."

A sad voice said, "There is one way that will convince him more certainly."

Thomas kept his face calm, though his stomach clenched. "Speak it."

"It shames and grieves me to say this, but if we gave *you* to him, he would grant us clemency."

That prompted irate words, but Thomas lifted his hands and voice. "Please, let me speak." The din subsided. "I, too, considered during the night whether I should offer myself to Duke Maerton. However, it would not be enough. He would also demand my heir. Thus, Esther and our child, and likely Jacob and Johanna, would also die. Only if I live, can I seek to protect my own, so we will depart. My letter makes it clear that I will remain in exile and never seek to harm the House of Fraetinloch."

"They will chase you the instant they see that bridge," a woman said.

A man chuckled. "That might take a little while."

Over the questions, Saul said, "There is a half-dead tree near the bridge, all swarming with wood ants. A breeze could topple it any day. Or a well-placed ax could bring it down on the bridge."

"Indeed," Thomas said, "if you care to show us any last kindness, I would ask the woodsmen among you to drop that tree after we leave."

Their assurance gave him comfort.

"What of Jacob's sister? Is she going with you?" That question sounded grim.

"Nay," Jacob said. "I know why you mistrust her, but she came here against her will and answered our questions when her husband snuck away. Him, I would not trust at all, but she claims he has fondness for her, so let her depart with him."

"Besides," Esther said, "we think that will show cooperation to the duke's men-at-arms, and perhaps, gain you a little favor."

It seemed that the group was coming to terms with the events, so Thomas said, "We bid you farewell now. 'Twould be best if you stay in your home sites as we leave."

"Fare you well," Esther said, then they hastened up the path.

The flurry of activity reminded Thomas of his departure from the castle. This time, all would walk except Esther, and even her mount carried a pack behind the saddle. They led the horses across the bridge one by one, then each family that accompanied him followed, every person laden with belongings or food.

Thomas gave the lead of Esther's horse to Jacob. "I shall follow you to the campsite." He climbed up a few limbs of a tree and found a place where he could keep watch. The last of the predetermined families crossed. Then others. Not good. Some, he didn't mind, but a few had consorted with the smugglers. At least they knew the bridge would be blocked, so perhaps they had decided to change their ways. He had no right to deny them anyway.

Some woodsmen waited for the bridge to clear, then set upon the weakened tree. Several bites of the ax, and the tree crashed down upon the far end of the bridge. Thomas had hoped it might break the bridge, but tower trees seemed invincible, even when dead. Still, the fallen tree wedged a limb in the cleft and reached more than halfway across. He couldn't have asked for a better blockade.

Thomas climbed down, raised a hand in thanks to the woodsmen, then followed his own. He jogged ahead when he could, though mostly they struggled over rocks and roots. Jacob was moving slow, for good reason, and Thomas caught up while they still journeyed to the campsite.

He helped Esther down from the saddle so Jacob could lead the horse under a low branch. "How do you fare, my love?"

"I am well."

She sounded tired, but she wouldn't want to hear that. They passed under the branch and he lifted her back into the saddle, then joined Jacob in the lead. Like everyone else in the caravan, Jacob asked about the tree.

"Aye," Thomas said. "It wedged a fat limb in the cleft. 'Twill be hard to clear, and I don't see how they can climb around it." He smiled as Esther murmured a prayer of thanks behind him. "The, uh, other news is that some extra families joined us. They must have worried the duke would see the tools they traded for."

Jacob grimaced. "The campsite is barely big enough for the ones we knew about."

Thomas was fast losing every worry. "A nuisance at first, but we'll have time to scout and spread out."

"You and Esther are getting the first livable cave we come to," Jacob declared.

Thomas laughed. "I know. And you and the midwife's family get the nearest shelters."

"Haven't we been through all this?" Esther asked, her voice lilting up.

Johanna led the pony right behind her and must have heard. "I swear my husband is more nervous than yours, Lady Esther."

Banter seemed to infect them all. Freedom from fear at last. Only now did Thomas realize how it had weighed on him. Struggles at the campsite didn't seem difficult. Nor did finding permanent shelter, though in truth, it was the hardest search yet. He had been sure that Esther would start labor the very day they crossed the river, but even that waited more than a week. Time enough for a couple scouts to journey to the crossing and back with news. One of Maerton's men had tried to cross the bridge despite the blockage and had fallen to his death. The duke had departed with his entire army and allowed families to return with him to Maerton Duchy. That suggested finality. At the very least, Thomas felt sure his letter would reach the king. They now had hope of peace.

When he shared the tidings with Esther, she wept tears of joy between early labor pains. Then the wait stretched long, while Thomas and Jacob fidgeted with simple tasks or paced on the flat ground that would someday support a house.

After several nerve-wracking hours, Johanna carried a bundle out of their newly chosen cave. "Your son, Lord Thomas."

He could only stare at first, but Johanna insisted he hold the fragile babe. "There now," she said. He must be doing it right, because she took a moment to enjoy the spectacle of him and the babe. "He looks just like you."

She returned to the cave, leaving him and Jacob staring after her. Thomas looked again at the tiny, sculpted face. "Does he?"

Jacob looked from him to the babe. "Nay."

Sunlight caught a swirl of hair, nigh invisible on the bald head. "I suppose he is blond, though." Thomas's slight movement caused the babe to open his eyes for a second or two. A new sort of warmth gathered in Thomas's chest. "His eyes are gray like mine."

"Aye. A little like you, then," Jacob said. A moment stretched. "Now what do you do with him?"

Good question. "Take him to his mother, because that is who I want to see anyway."

Thomas felt like he was invading a sanctum, but Esther's smile welcomed him, tired though she looked. "How fare you, my love?"

"Worry not," the midwife said, taking the babe from him. "She did well. You may talk with her for a few minutes, but then let her sleep."

Told what he could do with his own wife! At least the two other women were leaving. He settled beside Esther. "Now, perhaps, you can answer for yourself."

She uttered a tiny laugh. "I am well, Thomas."

"Mm. Didn't hurt at all, I suppose."

"Fine. I'm sore and tired, but I have the most beautiful babe in the world. I've thought of a name. Do...do you have one in mind?"

He shook his head. "I just won't name him after any of my ancestors."

"Oh. Do you have any ancestors named Nathan?"

"Nay. Why that name?"

"I found it in the holy book. He was an ordinary man who stood up to a king. That could have gotten him killed, but the king accepted truth because of his words. Besides..." The corners of her mouth quivered. "I like how it sounds."

"Then I am sure 'tis a fine name."

She sighed. "Nathan Kaituer."

He almost objected to the name that could get his son killed.

Words refused to form, so he tried to think of others, but her eyelids were falling. Maybe the midwife was right.

~

WHEN NATHAN WAS a couple weeks old, Thomas took his restless wife for an evening stroll to the cliff above the Great Sea. They donned their best clothes for the event. Though Esther carried their sleeping babe in a shawl wrapped snug against her chest, she was still his lovely bride.

He led her to the bench-like rock that he had padded with goatskin and sat with her to watch the sun set.

"Oh, this is lovely, Thomas! Thank you so much!"

"You're welcome, my love, but I didn't make it."

That drew her two-tone squeaky laugh, and she smiled up at him. "You made the moment, though. You just can't imagine how happy I am." She heaved an enormous sigh. "We've faced hard days and good days, but...I don't know why it is, but since we crossed the river, everything has changed."

"'Tis true."

She stared at the sinking sun. "Why do you think that is?"

"When we first crossed, I believed it was because we were safe. No longer hunted." He savored that freedom again. "In a way though, I know that no one is ever completely safe. It just doesn't seem to matter quite so much."

Far below them, waves caressed the rocks with a watery murmur. Nothing like the tumultuous River Vale on the day he'd learned of his family's fate. All the rage and betrayal and—he realized now—the grief. "I was going to throw my dagger into the River Vale on that awful day when...when I hated them all so bad. But I couldn't. I suppose a part of me remembered when my father gave it to me. The oldest son gets all the heirlooms, you know, but my father gave me that one. I never knew why. Maybe I still don't. He was always cold. Yet he kept me from... whatever his evil dealings were. Wouldn't let me into their discussions. Forbade me to leave the castle or even to walk the wall at night. Maybe he had promised my mother. I don't know. I often doubted that he loved her, but I think he did. I think maybe he cared about me too."

Thomas found himself shifting with the waves' rhythm. He hadn't meant to say all that. Did it have anything to do with what she'd asked? "I'll never like his final words, but he…" Thomas couldn't help but grin. "He *did* arrange a wonderful marriage for me—outrageous, though it was—and he sent me away to a fair land where we could start our own life, without all the burdens that the generations heaped upon us. Maybe… without even realizing, I have forgiven him, and…seen that there was something in him worthy of honor."

He blinked hard and swallowed to loosen his stupid constricting throat. "Anyway, that brings me peace." He shrugged. "I'm not sure what all that has to do with what you asked."

His favorite of her smiles formed in its slow, revealing way. "I didn't know before, but I do now. Your peace flows to me." Her gaze wandered out to sea. "I forgave them a while ago, for I didn't want to carry that weight. Now…now 'tis complete." She smiled at him again. "Forgiveness grants peace, and peace is stronger when it is shared."

SHARE THE ADVENTURE

I hope you found something in these pages that made your life a little richer. If you liked this story, maybe others would too. You can help them find it by leaving a brief review or even by clicking some stars wherever you like to purchase or review books. Those star ratings and reviews help me, too, and I greatly appreciate all of them.

Would you like to read more stories like this one? If so, I invite you to join my newsletter. I will send you some free short stories, share a little about life, and let you know about new books and an occasional sale. I won't overload your inbox or share your email address with others. You may unsubscribe at any time. Sign up at SharonRoseAuthor.com. I hope to hear from you!

BOOKS BY SHARON ROSE

FANTASY

Arts of Substance Trilogy:

To Form a Passage — Novel 1

To Weave the Wind — Novel 2

To Stream an Ocean — Novel 3

Castle in the Wilde Series:

A Castle Lost — An Early Days Novella

A Castle Sealed — Prequel Novella

A Castle Awakened — Novel 1

A Castle Contended — Novel 2

A Castle from Ashes — Novel 3

Castle in the Wilde — Trilogy Box Set

SCIENCE FICTION

Diverse Similarity — Novel 1

Diverse Demands — Novel 2

Agents of Rivelt — A Novel in Short Stories

More titles are coming. Get the latest news at SharonRoseAuthor.com.

ACKNOWLEDGMENTS

Again, I am delighted that my faithful team is still with me. You continue to create and encourage with the same giving spirit day after day, and month after month. With each book, more advance readers have joined me too. My appreciation for the many ways that you all help me continues to flow ever stronger. You make my heart smile!

There are too many of you to list by name, but when you see your group in the following paragraphs, just fill in your name because I'm thinking of you.

Family support is foundational to my writing. Husband, children, siblings, in-laws, even grandkids now. My thanks to all of you for everything from practical help, to encouragement, to just being your beautiful selves.

Bridgett Powers, my faithful editor and friend. Thanks for always being there for me. You know my books wouldn't be published without you—in more ways than one.

Kirk DouPonce, thank you for creating cover art that reflects the story-ideas bouncing around in my head. It is still always exciting to see how you turn my words into pictures.

Realm Makers—the conference, the online community, the people: This tribe, who understands both faith and speculative fiction, has made a huge difference in my author journey. And besides, you guys are just plain fun! Many thanks to all of you.

Write Now writer's group at Living Word Christian Center: You are delightful friends and encouragers. Thank you for listening to me read and giving me feedback.

Advance Readers: Though I will never see most of you face-to-face, the time you take to read, review, and spread the word, means more than you realize. Those of you who have sent me personal notes, your kind words always bring smiles to my face. And while I hate to admit that any tenacious, sneaky typos get this far, many thanks to the early readers who report those culprits to me.

To *all* of my readers: Even though these words are printed before you read this book, I feel as much gratitude for you as for everyone mentioned above. You've taken the time to walk through this fantasy world with me, and I don't take that for granted. I hope you've found something in it to bring light and hope to your days.

ABOUT THE AUTHOR

I started writing when I was seven years old. Okay, *My Life as a Flying Squirrel* may have had a couple spelling errors, but my classmates loved it.

Plenty of life has happened since that first story, and I've come to realize the things that fascinate me. People. Communication. Culture. Personality. Viewpoints. Beliefs. Anything that makes each of us beautifully unique. Small wonder that my art spills out in story form.

It was only a matter of time, before I just had to share my stories. I've published science fiction and now fantasy, two genres that allow us to explore reality while having fun.

When I'm not writing or reading, I may be traveling, enjoying gardens, or searching for unique coffee shops with my husband. We live in Minnesota, USA, famed for its mosquitoes —uh, I mean 10,000 lakes and vibrant seasons.

~

To find out more, visit SharonRoseAuthor.com.

Follow me on:
Amazon, Goodreads, BookBub, and Facebook.
Find all of my links at: https://linktr.ee/sharonrose.author